"I Don't Believe I Exist for You Except As Howard Carlton's Daughter."

"That's ridiculous."

"Is it? You can't deny that you knew it would upset my father if you and I became involved, can you?"

Brad leveled his troubled gaze on her. "I'd say he made that clear the night he took us to dinner."

She could actually see the color drain from his face as he took a step toward her, his hand outstretched, entreating. "Don't say anything more. You've made your point. There are insurmountable obstacles between you and me. I'll be seeing you, Claudia," he said tonelessly.

Claudia didn't see him leave because she was blinded by the tears she couldn't control. . . .

FRAN WILSON

is a woman of many talents and interests. She is a published writer of both fiction and non-fiction, has worked as an announcer and news reporter for a radio station, and has written music. She enjoys traveling, collecting Seri Indian wood carvings and refinishing antique furniture.

Dear Reader:

I'd like to take this opportunity to thank you for all your support and encouragement of Silhouette Romances.

Many of you write in regularly, telling us what you like best about Silhouette, which authors are your favorites. This is a tremendous help to us as we strive to publish the best contemporary romances possible.

All the romances from Silhouette Books are for you, so enjoy this book and the many stories to come.

Karen Solem
Editor-in-Chief
Silhouette Books

FRAN WILSON
Clouds Against the Sun

Silhouette Romance

Published by Silhouette Books New York

America's Publisher of Contemporary Romance

Gratefully, to Patricia

SILHOUETTE BOOKS
300 E. 42nd St., New York, N.Y. 10017

Copyright © 1985 by Fran Wilson
Cover artwork copyright © 1985 by Vicki Khuzami

Distributed by Pocket Books

ISBN: 0-373-08355-6

First Silhouette Books printing April, 1985

10 9 8 7 6 5 4 3 2 1

Map by Ray Lundgren

Books by Fran Wilson

Silhouette Romance

All joy is gone when love is done,
And dark clouds lie against the sun.

—F.E.W.

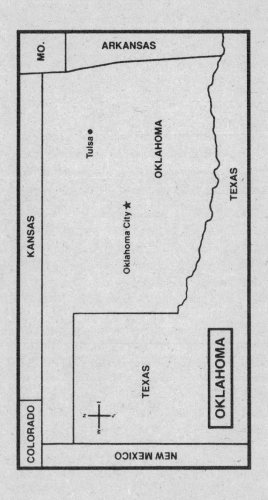

Chapter One

The tall framework of the derrick was a black silhouette against the prairie sky. A sky that on this April day was crystal clear and the color of bluets, the dainty, petite wild flowers that were just beginning to bloom in the dry clearings along the Oklahoma roadside.

Claudia's car rocked as her tires spewed the coarse sand and gravel of the recently graded county road. She eased her foot off the accelerator. Maybe if she slowed down to a crawl, she wouldn't feel as if she were riding one of those mechanical bulls. On a road like this she needed a car with sturdy shocks and luxury padded upholstery. Her small compact had neither.

Taking her eyes off the road long enough to glance at her wristwatch, she frowned. It had taken her longer than she'd thought it would to locate the site of this Stephens County well—the one that was being drilled adjacent to the Carlton Petroleum Corporation leases.

As she drove nearer, she saw a red and white pickup truck a short distance this side of the derrick, as well as a late-model copper-colored sports car. When she was within a few feet of the car, she saw that a man was sitting inside intently studying what appeared to be a map. He had the large sheet spread out across the steering wheel and strewn over the dashboard.

She parked her car nearby and got out. At the same time he pushed the paper aside, opened his door and ducked his head as he climbed out of the low bucket seat. Claudia noticed that his curly head all but matched his car, for his hair was sun streaked and the color of the red clay that forms the banks of Oklahoma's Cimarron River. He straightened and walked toward her. He was a tall, rangy man and suntanned as though he spent his life outdoors. His forehead was broad, his nose faintly arched.

"Hi. You looking for something or someone?" he asked, smiling upon her with admiring deference. He had the look of a born charmer of women who, by habit, smiles upon any girl who is not positively ugly in a manner that suggests he is already certain she will like him. Usually Claudia found this sort of approach annoying, but for some reason the warm approval in his rich brown eyes was pleasing to her.

"Both. I want to find someone who can tell me something about this well."

"Okay, you've found him. What is it you want to know?"

"Any information you're allowed to give out. You see, I work for Carlton Petroleum Corporation in Tulsa. They hold leases on a block of land adjacent to this area."

"Carlton!" His expression altered and a nerve twitched along his jaw as his chin jutted slightly forward. "Pardon an old cliché, but what's a woman like you doing tramping around leases?''

"I like to see things for myself. After all, this is a hot area. You know that. There have been a number of successful wells in the same geological formation you're drilling into.'' She pulled off her dark glasses as she talked and leveled intelligent blue-gray eyes on his face.

"You know a lot about geological formations?'' he asked.

"I know enough.''

He studied her now with interest as well as amusement. "Don't tell me you're a geologist!''

"No, I'm a petroleum engineer,'' she answered matter-of-factly, but she couldn't keep from smiling because her statement obviously was the last thing he had expected to hear from her.

He grinned at her good-naturedly. "Well, I guess there's nothing that says a woman can't be beautiful, blond and brainy all at the same time.''

She tried to appear unaware of his flattering words and eyes. "Now that we've covered the subject of my job training, could you tell me whatever figures your boss lets you release about this well?''

He crossed his arms across his chest, studying her thoughtfully. "That depends on who's asking and why they want to know. What's your job at Carlton?''

"I'm in the land department.''

"Then you're looking to lease more land around here?''

"We will if we can.''

"Is your company planning to drill?'' There was cool speculation now in the look he gave her.

"I thought I was the one who wanted to ask questions.'' Claudia slanted her smiling eyes at him.

He returned her smile. "All right, you ask them, but I hope you're not as curious as you are pretty." He leaned forward, bending his head closer to hers.

Claudia thrust her sunglasses on again as if she felt it necessary to put up a guard against him, then walked a few steps away and peered out toward the well site. "How far down have you gone?"

"Fifty-two hundred feet."

"Did you get a show of oil or gas in the shallow zone?"

"We tested two areas. Nothing was commercial," he said tersely.

Turning, she shot him a curious look. "How do you feel it's going?"

"I expect to hit pay in another week." There was more than just a hint of finality in his clipped words. Claudia gathered he was not about to divulge any further information about the drilling of this particular well. He had been pleasant, but it was apparent that he considered she had no business hanging around a well that her company had no part in. Petroleum engineer or not, this man saw her as an intruder.

"I appreciate the information. Thanks for taking time to talk to me."

"Anytime," he said with a casual shrug, but he was frowning and seemed to be scrutinizing her intently just as he had earlier. What was it about her that bothered him? she wondered.

She turned, heading back to her car, but he followed after her. "Wait a minute," he said, taking hold of her arm. "I'll make a deal with you. Tell me your name, and I'll give you easy directions for getting back to the main highway from here."

"Oh, I should have told you before," she said, turning

her eyes up at him and smiling her apology. "I'm Claudia Carlton."

His hand fell abruptly away from her arm, his keen eyes narrowing. "I sure never figured that."

She gave him an uncertain look. "What do you mean?"

"First you tell me you're a petroleum engineer. Now I find out that you're Howard Carlton's daughter. Do you have any more surprises up your sleeve?"

"None that I can think of."

"Good. I find that quite enough for one day."

Claudia studied the expression on his tanned face, the determined set of his jaw, the agate hardness that now marked his brown eyes.

He cleared his throat harshly. "Did your father send you out here to find out about this particular drilling operation?"

"Not this more than any other. I'm looking at everything in the area near Carlton holdings," she said evenly, determined to keep her cool with this testy man. She was darned if she could understand why finding out who she was should make him so defensive.

The tall redhead turned his head sharply, looking back over his shoulder at a car that was heading down the road, stirring up a cloud of dust as it came. "Damn, that's Sam, I'll bet," he said more to himself than to Claudia. He immediately stepped around her and yanked open her car door so she could slide into the driver's seat. His actions made it clear that he wanted her out of the way before this Sam person arrived on the scene. "Circle out to the left when you back around. You'll escape the boss's dust that way." He closed the door quickly after her; then, keeping his hands on the ledge of the open window, he thrust his head down close to hers. "Take the gravel road back about four miles until you come to the junction with the blacktop. Turn right and go north. It'll lead you right to the main highway.''

The oncoming car drove up on the far side of the red pickup just as Claudia started her motor. She put her car in reverse and swung back and around, making a wide arc. Before she drove away, she glanced over to see a rugged lumberjack of a man unfold his large frame from his car, wave his broad hand toward the younger man and holler, ''What are you up to, Brad?''

The newcomer strode across the few yards that separated them and immediately the two of them fell into conversation. Seeing them standing together, Claudia noticed that they were the same height and even resembled each other to some degree. Their bodies looked lean and hard, with long thighs, so that as they stood together they were both straight as spears. Also, both men had the same copper red hair, although Sam's was liberally touched with white.

Claudia paused another moment, speculating about the two drillers. Then she rolled up the window against the dust and drove away.

''Don't tell me that you've got a girl now who follows you out to the field?'' the older man asked, his hazel eyes dancing with amusement.

''Strictly business with this one, Dad,'' Brad answered his father, no trace of a smile on his face. ''What's more, it's going to set you back on your heels when I tell you who that good-looking blond was.''

''From the glimpse I caught of her, I'd say she's shapely enough to be a Dallas Cowboy cheerleader, but from your grim expression I take it she wasn't out here to practice cheers.''

"That's for sure." Brad scowled. "Her name is Claudia Carlton. She's Howard Carlton's daughter."

Sam's heavy brows came together in a bar above his glowering eyes. "What the hell was a Carlton doing on a lease where my rigs are drilling?"

"Scouting the area, was what she said. She didn't know who I was and I didn't tell her my name. I'm sure she took me for a tool pusher."

"What reason did she offer for inspecting our site?" Sam snapped, his face colored with anger.

"Carlton Petroleum evidently holds leases on the section east of here. At least that's what she claimed."

"You believe that?"

"No reason not too. She's a petroleum engineer and works for her father in the land department. It follows she'd be checking out the activity."

"Yeah, I guess so." He pushed his breath out through his clenched teeth, making a harsh rasping sound. "I'm damn glad you didn't volunteer any information that she might take back to Howard. He doesn't need to know Alamo Drilling Company has the contract on this well. Anyway, that double-crossing Carlton doesn't want to hear the name of Hayes any more than I want to hear Carlton. It's been like that for eighteen years now, and it will be for another fifty as far as I'm concerned." Sam Hayes turned away sharply and started walking in the direction of the drilling rig. "I came out to see the core samples that were taken," he called back over his shoulder. "After that I'm heading home to Abilene."

Brad stared after his father's broad-shouldered back. What a proud, tough, remarkable man he was. Eighteen years was a long time, but not long enough for his father to get over what his onetime friend, Howard Carlton, had tried to do to him. And for no reason that Sam could ever find out—that was the strange part of it.

Brad continued to gaze after his father, his forehead creased in a thoughtful frown. Sam hadn't spoken about Howard Carlton for a long time now. Brad wished that he hadn't told him who the girl was. If he hadn't mentioned her name, neither of them would be recalling what had happened eighteen years ago.

Brad had been eleven, nearly twelve that summer, an impressionable age to experience a complete change of life-style, much less accept it. He felt a constriction in his chest at the thought of what that change had meant to his father, his mother and to him. It wasn't just that they'd had to move out of Tulsa, the city where he had been born and had always lived. It also meant leaving the big, red brick house with the stately white pillars across the front and the fenced backyard shaded by giant elms where his friends had gathered to play with him. Even now after so many years, the word *home* and that house in Tulsa were synonymous in Brad's mind.

During those years in Tulsa, Sam Hayes and Howard Carlton had been good friends and had worked together, Howard using Sam's rigs for all the wells Carlton Petroleum Corporation drilled in Oklahoma. The arrangement had proved financially profitable for both men.

Early in the summer of that year, without apparent cause or reason, Howard suddenly ceased using Sam's drilling rigs, and as rapidly as he could he turned over all his business to other drilling contractors. When Sam tried to discover the reason for this break between them, Howard refused to see him or discuss his actions with him.

The loss of Carlton's business placed Sam Hayes in severe financial straits. He was forced to leave Tulsa and seek out new drilling contracts with other oil companies in

Texas. This was no minor setback. It was near disaster. Howard Carlton had for some unknown reason set out to ruin Sam Hayes, and he very nearly succeeded. It took endless months before Sam had even one of his rigs working again.

Brad stood motionless, still looking out toward the drilling rig. His troubled eyes were not seeing the dark steel derrick, however. Rather he was reviewing a mental image of his mother's sad, haunted face during those troubled months. In a number of ways Elizabeth Hayes suffered more than anyone else as a result of what Howard Carlton had caused to happen. She had been in the early months of a long-hoped-for pregnancy. Worry over their grave financial losses and the pain of being forced to give up the home she loved came, unfortunately, at a crucial time in her pregnancy. Elizabeth lost her baby.

Remembering his mother's suffering and unhappiness, Brad swore under his breath. He wished that he had not been there that afternoon when Claudia Carlton happened along. Too bad that a woman with such a charming, gamine face and with that appealing cleft in her chin had to bear the name of Carlton. Otherwise, she had a lot going for her. He rammed his right hand into his pocket and strode off to join his father. He could even believe that Howard Carlton's daughter might not be a half-bad petroleum engineer.

For the next few weeks Claudia thought about little else than the area she'd looked at on that April afternoon. She even found herself reflecting on the good-looking but rather ambivalent-acting man she had met.

She had worked diligently these past weeks to obtain leases on the areas surrounding the Carlton properties. Three acreage owners had already signed and returned lease contracts. Now it seemed the only outstanding mineral right she needed to lease was one owned by El-Sa Corporation in Texas. Claudia had directed a letter to El-Sa but had received no response. Several days ago she had telephoned, reaching only an answering service. She left a message asking that someone from El-Sa return her call at the first opportunity. She had heard nothing.

On Wednesday morning, the second week in May, Claudia had just arrived at her desk when her telephone began to ring. When she answered, a man's pleasant deep voice informed her he was returning her call to his company concerning the leasing of acreage in an Oklahoma area.

Claudia began rapidly shuffling through the papers on top of her desk with her free hand, wanting to locate the file she had started on the property owned by this Texas corporation.

"I'd like to set up a time to discuss a lease of your mineral rights in Stephens County," she said. "I'll fly to Texas and meet with you whenever you say."

There was a lengthy pause, and for a moment she was afraid he might object to seeing her. "I'd be glad to talk with you about this," he offered finally, "but I'm seldom here at my home base. What do you say I meet with you in your office in Tulsa on Friday morning? I could make it at ten-thirty."

"That would be fine—just fine." Her surprise showed in her voice. After the difficulty she had had getting in contact with this Texan, she couldn't quite believe he was now arranging a meeting that would prove so convenient for her. "By all means, Friday morning then," she reiterated, smiling into the phone.

"Right. I'll be looking forward to that, Miss Carlton."

Claudia realized that he had hung up. She took the

phone away from her ear and, still holding it in her hand, stared down at the receiver curiously. Something bothered her about this, but for the life of her, she couldn't figure out what it could be. This man who represented El-Sa sounded agreeable, more than that, quite cooperative. Wasn't he coming to Tulsa rather than have her make a trip to Texas to see him? Surely this indicated that there was every possibility of making an amiable agreement between El-Sa and Carlton. Why then did she suddenly feel apprehensive?

She pressed the receiver back in its cradle and stood up. Turning her back to her desk, she looked out the one oversized window in her small cubicle of an office. Though she was the boss's daughter, she was still junior to the other engineers at Carlton. Her office was tasteful and adequate and that was about all you could say for it. Located on the fourth floor of the steel, concrete and glass high-rise that was the Carlton Building, Claudia could look out through her wide window and view the sidewalks and streets four stories below. At the moment the mid-morning sounds of metropolitan Tulsa filtered in through the plate glass. As she stared down at the traffic in the street below her, she was only vaguely conscious of the stream of cars, the periodic blare of their horns and the continuous churning and hissing of their tires. She remained caught up in her thoughts of her Friday meeting with the Texan. Who and what was this El-Sa Corporation?

The phone on her desk rang again, interrupting her speculations.

"Hi, honey." Her father's exuberant voice caused Claudia to hold the receiver slightly away from her ear. "I've got to leave town in the morning and I'll be gone for several days, so I wanted to touch base with you. Thought

I'd like to take my favorite daughter out to dinner at the Financial Club tonight.''

"I'd like that too. The food is great, and I saw where they're featuring dinner music and entertainment. I'll dress up,'' she responded enthusiastically. "In fact, it gives me an excuse to buy the aquamarine dress I resisted last week.''

Howard laughed. "You resisted a new dress? I don't believe it.''

"You'd believe it if I told you the price. It's absurdly expensive for a girl on my salary to even consider.''

"Are you hitting on me for a raise, or hinting that you want me to buy the dress for you?'' he asked in what Claudia recognized as his indulgent-father tone.

She gave a quick, happy laugh. "Neither one, so you can relax. But don't think I don't appreciate the offer. I happen to be quite solvent at the moment, so I can splurge and have this silk dress. It's elegant and I'm worth it,'' she added gaily. "I'll wear it tonight. What time?''

"How about seven-thirty?''

"Fine. Shall I come down to your apartment?''

"No, I'll pick you up. It's easier.''

Claudia realized her father was right. The Financial Club was located on the top floor of one of Tulsa's suburban banks and was much closer to the apartments where she lived than it was to the near downtown location of the Club Tower apartments, where her father had lived ever since he and her mother were divorced several years ago.

At the time of their divorce, the beautiful home where Claudia had grown up was sold because Vanessa Carlton had been much more interested in a large cash settlement than in keeping and maintaining the spacious Carlton house. Claudia was away in college, so she had to agree that it didn't make good sense for her mother to hold on to a large house. Although she admitted that it made her sad to realize that she probably would never again step inside the home where she had lived for the first eighteen years of her life.

Claudia's face contorted with pain as one sad recollection ended and another, more tragic one took its place. It was while she was still at the university that her mother had died. How the thought of it hurt. It was painful enough that her incredibly beautiful mother had not lived beyond the age of forty, but Claudia hated having to remember the salacious scandal that had surrounded the car accident that took her mother's life and that of Vanessa's latest lover. Never one to employ discretion in her numerous affairs, Vanessa had involved herself in a relationship with a prominent politician who happened also to be married. When they were killed together while spending a clandestine weekend at a resort hotel in Scottsdale, Arizona, the resulting publicity left ugly scars to mar her father's life and Claudia's as well. She was haunted by the fear that she might be like her mother. Surely that couldn't be possible. She would never let it be.

Abruptly Claudia pushed her chair back and sprang to her feet. She had a dress to buy on her lunch hour. She had better be on her way.

After eating a club sandwich at the colorful cafe in the center of the Utica Square shopping mall, she returned to the specialty shop and sighed with relief when she discovered the aquamarine crepe de chine dress had not been sold. Trying it on again, she fingered the becoming high ruffled neck and the interesting button detail of the bodice. She wondered how she'd been strong enough to resist buying it the first time. It was perfect for her because of its conservative styling as well as its subtle pastel color. Claudia knew she was going to love wearing this dress. She was particularly conscious of the fact that this was a dress totally different from anything her mother would have ever worn. This seemed important to her, probably more so today because earlier she had been thinking so much about Vanessa.

Vanessa Carlton had always chosen every garment she wore with one object in mind—to call attention to her flagrant, sensuous beauty. She had dressed to attract men, for she had an insatiable desire to be admired and pursued. Her husband's love and attention seemed never enough to satisfy her. For Vanessa, taking lovers became a way of life, eventually a way to death as well.

Claudia looked at her image in the three-way mirror in the dressing room. She was different from her mother, wasn't she? She must make sure that she was.

Removing the blue silk dress, she handed it to the saleswoman who'd been helping her. "I'll take it," she said decisively, her eyes more vividly blue than usual. "I believe the color of this dress is the prettiest I've ever seen," she said with a smile. "Anyway, blue is my favorite color."

It was raining Friday morning as Claudia drove to work. The apartment complex where she lived was located on the southern outskirts of Tulsa, and stormy weather slowed the flow of traffic, so it took her almost forty minutes that morning to reach the center of the city. Spring rains, though frequent, were seldom long-lasting. By the time she reached the Carlton Building the sky had begun to lighten and fragile rays of sunshine appeared.

Claudia had the file on the Stephens County leases in readiness for the ten-thirty appointment with the Texan. She had been anticipating the meeting and she hoped the man representing El-Sa would be prompt. It irritated her that she had not gotten his name when they spoke on the telephone. Now, unless he told her immediately when he came into the office, she would have to ask him. It was probably just an idiosyncracy of hers, but she found it awkward in a business situation to have to ask a man his name. This man knew her name from her letter and from his answering service; not knowing his put her at a disadvantage.

Circling her desk, she went to the door of her office and glanced out at the wall clock next to the elevators. Comparing the time with her own watch, she found them in agreement. That meant she had twenty-five minutes to wait, enough time to take the memo she'd prepared to the legal department. Stepping back inside her office, she reached over her desk for the sheet of paper she needed. The quick, careless movement of her arm knocked the Stephens County file off the side of her desk, strewing papers across the carpet. She knelt down, her back toward the door, and started gathering up what had spilled out of the file.

"Let me give you a little help there, Miss Carlton."

She heard the hearty male voice at the same time as she felt a pair of strong hands under her arms, lifting her up. He turned her around, and now his warm hands spanned her slender waist. Claudia found herself looking into familiar brown eyes, which sparkled with obvious enjoyment at discovering her in this present predicament. Her blue eyes widened, and she raised them to view his head of sandy red hair, confirming what she already knew. The man whose firm hands secured her midriff was the one she had talked to at the drilling rig a few weeks ago. She stood there gaping at him, too surprised to utter a word.

He inclined his head so it was just inches away from her upturned face. "You were expecting me, I'm sure, Claudia. You see, I'm Brad Hayes." Smiling, he lowered his face even closer. "Vice-president of El-Sa," he added with an amused chuckle.

Chapter Two

Claudia not only heard his astounding words, but she felt them. Their closeness was almost an embrace, and his breath stirred the wisps of her wheat-colored hair where it curled softly forward at her temple.

Struggling for a semblance of businesslike composure, she stepped back away from him, pulling herself from his grasp. "Well, Brad Hayes, like they say, it really *is* a small world, isn't it?" She tossed her words out, trying to sound off hand. "And since you said that the man who drove up to your rig as I was leaving that day was your boss, am I right in believing he's the president of your corporation?"

Brad's expression sobered. "Correct. That was my father, Sam Hayes." He paused, looking at her intently.

She surmised that he expected her to comment on his statement, but at the moment she couldn't figure out what he expected her to say. The name Sam Hayes meant nothing to her, and she couldn't recall having heard it before. She smiled, hunching her shoulders in a slight shrug. "You and I are alike in that respect then. We both work for our fathers." She quickly returned the conversation to business by inquiring, "Please, tell me about El-Sa. What type of corporation is it?"

"Actually, it's a holding company which owns stock in two operating companies, Hayes Oil Field Supply Company and Alamo Drilling."

Her face wore a quizzical expression. "How do you get El-Sa from Hayes and Alamo?"

"You don't. You get it from Elizabeth and Sam, my parents' names."

"I see." She gave him a comprehending smile. "El-Sa is really a family incorporation."

Brad's face remained sober and his voice matched his expression. "We Hayeses are a closely united family and always have been. You'll discover we're one for all and all for one."

"Like the three musketeers," she countered lightly, but her smile faded. He was totally serious about his family and their business operations. For some reason, she got the feeling that she'd missed something that she should understand in order to get on the right business footing with this man. Pivoting on her heel, she turned away from him and moved quickly around behind her desk. "Pull up my one visitor's chair, Brad," she said, pointing to the chrome and vinyl chair, which was placed next to the filing cabinet at one side of the square room.

He looked over where she indicated, then followed her suggestion, drawing the chair up in front of her desk and taking his seat. "Are you telling me that when you contacted us you were not aware that Sam Hayes owned any of the companies involved in El-Sa?'' he asked, looking her squarely in the face.

Claudia frowned, wondering why he was making so much of this. ''I didn't even know there *was* a Sam Hayes—or a Brad Hayes, either—until you told me just now, but I will say that I'm glad the man who answered my questions at the drilling site and Brad Hayes of El-Sa turned out to be one and the same.'' She inclined her head, smiling at him beguilingly. ''And to answer your question further, I learned El-Sa owned the mineral rights on the property Carlton is interested in leasing by consulting Mid-Continent Map Company. That's all the information I asked for, so it's all they gave me.''

As Brad listened to her explanation, he rubbed his suntanned hand along the side of his jaw, his eyes narrowing like a cat's. ''I thought your father might have made some comments to you. You see, anyone who's been around the oil business as long as your dad and mine, knows the names of men in drilling and supply companies throughout the Southwest.''

''Maybe my father does, but he's out of town this week and I haven't mentioned leasing your specific property to him.'' Arching her brows, she added wryly, ''Honestly, Brad, since you work for your own father too, I'd think you'd understand what great satisfaction it will give me if I'm able to present a fait accompli to the boss.'' She smiled again. ''I admit that I haven't been working for the company all that long yet. I'm still trying to prove to my father that I'm a smart woman who can get the job done on her own power.'' Tossing her head back, she gave a quick, light laugh, then cleared her throat to indicate she intended now to get down to business. ''What do you say we discuss terms and figures and see if I can make an agreement with you?'' She opened the file, which she had retrieved from the floor, and set the papers in order.

Brad watched her, a curious glint in his eyes and a twisted smile marking his mouth.

As they talked for the next hour and a half, Claudia realized that they were far from any agreement on the terms of the lease. She surmised that Brad would probably agree to the three-sixteenth royalty she offered, but the figure that he had in his mind for the amount of the lease bonus was vastly higher than the top figure she had been authorized to offer.

Tension built up inside of her, and she had the distinct feeling that she was not handling the negotiations well. She couldn't put her finger on what it was, but something in Brad Hayes's attitude toward each point she brought up made her feel defensive. At one point she wondered if it was because she was a woman. Did he resent dealing with a female petroleum engineer? Was he determined not to make any concessions to her, and would he then insist that this deal be handled by the top man in the land department, or even by Howard Carlton himself?

Suddenly she realized her mind had been wandering and that she hadn't said anything for several minutes. Glancing across the desk, she felt heat rise in her face. Brad was watching her intently.

''Let's see now,'' she murmured lamely. ''Let's discuss—''

''Let's not,'' he interrupted. ''I think we should put this discussion on hold while I take you to lunch.'' He rose immediately from his chair, not allowing her to offer an objection.

A wave of relief washed over her and she sighed audibly, glad that he had been the one to bring their office conversation to an end. "It has gotten to be lunchtime, hasn't it?" What an inane remark, she thought the second she'd said it. Lowering her head quickly, she tugged open the bottom drawer of her desk and lifted out her purse. When she looked up again Brad was carrying his chair back, placing it against the wall by the filing cabinet.

"There's one important thing I should have made clear at the outset, Claudia, and that is that I make it a practice to get to know all about a person before I do business with him—" He grinned. "With her, that is. You don't mind if I start learning about you over lunch, do you?"

"Not if I get the answers to the questions I have about you at the same time." She smiled, and walked around her desk to join him. Already she was feeling on a little better footing with him. Lunch and a bit of socializing could be the answer. It was apparent that she hadn't achieved much of a rapport with Brad by sitting on the other side of an office desk from him. Maybe she'd find that the two of them could relate better across a table for two in one of Tulsa's good restaurants.

Brad's tanned face was lit by an easy smile as his hand glided under her elbow, taking hold of her arm with practiced ease. "You know, getting to know a pretty blond petroleum engineer is apt to prove the most interesting thing I've done in a long time." His brown eyes caressed her with a look that tinted her cheeks. It was more than just what his eyes told her; it was experiencing the vibrations, the unmistakable electricity that was there between them. It unnerved her. Sudden feelings of strong attraction for a man she'd spoken with for less than two hours was a totally new experience for her.

The down elevator was well filled with passengers from the upper floors by the time it reached them. Brad stepped on after Claudia, and the two of them took a space that was suited for only one. Of necessity her body was pressed warmly against the side of his, and she was aware of the pleasing rich scent of tobacco mixed with after-shave. "You smoke a pipe, don't you?" she whispered.

"Sometimes," he whispered back. "When I'm driving on the road or inspecting a well site. What made you ask? Can you feel my pipe in my coat pocket?"

"No, I'm numb from being packed in here like a sardine."

The elevator reached the lobby and they stepped off. As they left the building, Brad searched his pocket and extracted a dark briarwood pipe, which he handed to Claudia. "This is my favorite pipe. I was smoking it on the way up from Abilene. I forgot I'd put it in my pocket because I usually leave it in the car. Do you object to men smoking?"

"Cigars I do, but I don't mind this. In fact, I think there's something manly and appealing about a man smoking a pipe." She handed it back to him.

"I'll remember that." He smiled and took her arm. "At the right time, I'll even remind you that you said it."

Brad had left his car in the parking arcade near the Carlton Building. As he and Claudia drove through the exit gate, Brad turned into the southbound traffic lane. "The last time I was in Tulsa on business I ate at a great little French restaurant at London Square. I thought we'd have lunch there unless there's somewhere else you'd prefer."

"As a matter of fact that's perfect," she answered, shifting around, settling herself more comfortably into the spoon-shaped leather seats of Brad's foreign car. "Actually ideal for me. Dad uses the flower shop there in London Square, and when he left town he told me to take care of ordering flowers to mark Myra Allan's anniversary with the company. She's been my father's loyal and dedicated secretary for twenty years come next Monday, so she deserves having special notice made of the occasion.''

Brad's bold profile altered slightly as he thrust his chin forward. "Twenty years," he muttered under his breath.

Claudia inclined her head toward him. "What'd you say?''

He glanced at her, frowning. "Nothing, I was thinking about your Myra Allan. If she's been with Carlton Petroleum for twenty years, she'd remember Sam.''

"How's that?''

"Dad started his first drilling company right here in Tulsa, and twenty years ago he was still working here. He would have been in and out of your dad's office a good deal, I expect.''

Her face reflected her surprise. "You mean our fathers know each other?''

"They knew each other then," he said tersely.

Before she could ask him anything further, he wheeled the car sharply into the tree-edged parking area at London Square. The English-style architecture made the shop fronts, with their leaded windows glimmering darkly against soft gray stone, look like a charming scene from Victorian London.

Claudia stopped first at the florist and ordered an arrangement of pink and white carnations interspersed with stalks of blue Dutch iris. Rejoining Brad, she found he had already arranged for their table at La Cuisine and ordered a glass of white wine for her to sip while she listened to the waiter recite the menu for the day.

Claudia made up her mind quickly, choosing one of the specialties of the house, chicken salad served with slices of avocado and sections of Mandarin oranges. Claiming that a salad was not hearty enough for him, Brad ordered the boeuf bourguignon. When the waiter disappeared to place their order, Brad lifted his wine glass and touched it to Claudia's.

"What do you say we drink to our first lunch date and to getting to know the whys, whats and wherefores about each other?"

"I'll drink to that, but I shouldn't because we're not starting out even. You have an advantage over me."

"How do you figure that?"

"You already seem to know a great deal about me and my family, while I know scarcely anything about you." Claudia took another taste of her wine, eyeing Brad thoughtfully over the rim of her glass.

"Well, let's see if I can't remedy that." He leaned forward, resting one arm on the table. "To begin at the beginning, I was born on a dark and stormy night in January, approximately twenty-nine and a half years ago." He employed a melodramatic tone of voice, and his coffee-colored eyes sparkled with amusement. "That means I'm under the sign of Capricorn, the goat."

"I should have known, or at least guessed about the goat. That explains why you met me head on over the terms of the lease this morning. That goat symbol means you're argumentative," she teased, smiling.

He shook his head. "You're wrong. It actually signifies persistence. If you study the ancient astrologers, the symbol for Capricorn was the sea-goat, a sprightly animal with front feet on dry land and hind feet formed like the tail of a fish or a mermaid. Wishing to dash headlong up the road to success, the sea-goat is detained by its fishlike tail, and in order to make progress he must strive persistently over a long period of time."

She looked askance. "You made that whole thing up, now admit it."

"Read about the signs of the zodiac if you won't believe me." Picking up his napkin, he squared his chair in front of his place. The waiter had brought their lunch, and he served the attractive plates with a Continental flourish.

Before she lifted her fork, Claudia was determined to get in a final word. "I'm not a Capricorn like you, but I am persistent. I'm also acquisitive, and I want to acquire that lease from El-Sa."

"No talking business during lunch. That's my rule of the day, remember?" He offered her a smile filled with his brand of masculine charm. "Besides, I was under the impression that you wanted to hear all about *me* over lunch."

"Oh, I do, I really do!" Claudia exaggerated her words with dramatic emphasis. "Please continue and tell me what happened after you were born under the sign of Capricorn."

He had begun to eat his lunch. Now he paused, glanced over at her and laughed. "You did ask for this, you know. Shall I tell you about the years between cradle and first grade, or shall I skip right to puberty?"

Spontaneous laughter burst from her lips. At the nearby tables, heads turned and at least eight pairs of eyes leveled on her and Brad. Self-consciously, she grabbed her napkin from her lap and pressed it hard against her mouth, stifling her laughter.

"I really didn't say anything that funny," Brad whispered huskily.

She uncovered her mouth, disclosing sober, compressed lips. Her eyes, however, still mirrored her amusement. "I'm sorry, Brad, but I have to admit that the image of you as a redheaded adolescent going through voice changes struck me as really funny. But you can spare me that period; I assure you I've no intention of revealing anything about my own awkward years to you.''

He reached across the table, touching the tips of her fingers where her hand rested beside her plate. ''I doubt you ever had any. If you did, you grew out of them beautifully.''

''That's a nice thing to say. Thank you.'' She picked up her fork, mainly as a prop because she felt the need of something to occupy her hands. ''So, tell me how long you've been in business with your father?''

''When I finished college, I went right to work for Alamo Drilling.'' He paused and waited for her to look at him before adding, ''I've a degree in petroleum engineering too, you know.'' A suggestion of a smile dimpled the corners of his mouth.

Claudia smiled back at him. ''I guessed that this morning when you were questioning every point in the lease agreement. Were you trying to get back at me because I took you for a tool pusher that first afternoon?''

Brad shook his head. ''No, that never bothered me. I was a tool pusher before I was a vice-president. When you work for Sam Hayes he sees you have on-the-job experience in every aspect of the drilling business.'' His easy shrug accompanied a low chuckle. ''Being his son and having a college degree didn't earn me any different treatment.''

''I'll bet you and your father are a good deal alike.''

''I'd be glad if we were.''

''That afternoon when I saw the two of you standing together, I thought that you resembled each other.''

''Two copperheads,'' he quipped. ''But that doesn't mean either of us is a snake in the grass or poisonous,'' he added jokingly.

She didn't comment, but continued to regard him

thoughtfully. Red hair and quick tempers went together. She wondered if that was going to prove true with Brad. From what she'd seen so far, he was shrewd about his business dealings, but he maintained good humor about it. To keep on the safe side, however, she intended not to provoke him if she could avoid it.

"You got awfully quiet all of a sudden," he said, looking at her quizzically. "You don't like my copperhead pun, is that it? You prefer dark and handsome men to rugged redheads, I'll bet. That's just my luck." He feigned a woebegone expression, which made her smile.

"I prefer a Capricorn who will stop putting me off and tell me what I have to do to get him to come to terms on a lease with Carlton," she said, her eyes smiling but her voice firm and completely serious. "And really, Brad, since we've already taken more than an hour for this delightful lunch, don't you think we had better get back to my office?"

He signaled the waiter for their check. "I'll tell you what I think we should do." He narrowed his eyes, smiling wryly. "But let's talk about it when we get back to the car."

Claudia studied his expression, frowning. Now what did he have in mind? she wondered. Was he going to put her off, procrastinate about giving her a decision on the lease? She got the feeling that was exactly what his manner implied. She'd almost bet that he had no intention of discussing it any further that afternoon. That thought gave rise to a feeling of irritation. Brad Hayes was as devious as he was charming. He seemed to be playing some kind of game with her, but what kind? And why?

Pushing her chair back, she jumped to her feet. "I'll just go put on fresh lipstick while you're waiting on the check. I'll catch up with you at the car." With those few

words, she excused herself and left the table for the ladies'
room. She had been afraid to sit there with him another
minute for fear she'd lose her cool. She found Brad Hayes
was a new experience for her. He had a magnetism and
vitality that set him apart from other men she'd dealt with.
She knew she was attracted to him, but she was also
exasperated by him. She had to admit that he did have a
disarming way about him. Maybe it had something to do
with his looks. Did a certain type of personality accompa-
ny Brad's combination of copper-colored hair and rich
brown eyes? She smiled inwardly. He was different from
any blond or dark-haired man she'd dated, and she found
that fact intrigued her.

In the bathroom she inclined her head close to the
mirror and applied fresh lipstick automatically, her mind
still on Brad. "Copperhead," she muttered under her
breath. He'd joked about the label he'd given himself,
declaring it didn't mean he was a snake who'd poison her.
But he hadn't said he wouldn't bite. The mirror reflected
an impish gleam in the depths of her blue eyes. Well—
there was nothing to keep her from biting back, was there?

The rising wind was causing the trees to sway and dip
their leafy branches in a nature ballet. As Claudia and
Brad returned to his car, she looked up at the darkening
sky. It appeared as if the morning rain might be returning
after all. As she bent over to climb in the car, a gust of
wind caught her hair, tousling it. She attempted to smooth
it with her hands as Brad slid into the seat on his side.

Leaning over, he raised his hand to her face, pushing
back the soft blond hair the wind had blown across her
forehead. He allowed his fingers to linger for a moment in
the silky strands before they slid caressingly across her

cheek. "Whoever said the most beautiful women were in Texas never saw a wind-tossed Oklahoma girl."

She would have considered his words part of his charming male line, except he was looking at her seriously, his eyes reflecting the same flattering compliment as his words. Too, there was something more in his searching look than just the interest a man displays in an attractive woman. Disconcerted, Claudia was relieved when he stopped touching her face. His touch had an unsettling effect on her. Oddly, she still could feel a tingling sensation along the arch of her cheek where his fingers had traced their warm path.

Brad pushed the key in the ignition, but he did not immediately start the car. "I'll drive you back downtown and drop you off at your building if you say I must, but I really want you to go over to Lake Keystone with me."

Claudia's surprise showed on her face. "You're going to Keystone now, this afternoon?"

Brad nodded. "I have to go to a real estate office there before it closes at three o'clock. While I'm on business here in Tulsa I'm going to use a friend's place there on the lake. But the woman who handles it for him and who'll give me the key closes her office when her children get out of school at three."

Hearing his explanation, Claudia automatically glanced down at her wristwatch. "Then I'd say you'd better get going. It's two now."

He smiled, looking pleased. "I take it that means you're coming with me." He flipped the ignition switch and the motor responded in an instantaneous hum of power.

Claudia's eyes crinkled in a demure smile. "It's against my better judgment, but I'll go." She watched him as he took his pipe out of his pocket and put it in his mouth, not lighting it, just holding it firmly between his teeth. "You know, of course, that I should insist on getting back to work. I think that you're leading me astray," she said, laughing.

Removing his pipe for a moment, he teased her with a leer. "I intend to give it my best try."

Unable to think of a sharp comeback, Claudia pretended to ignore his remark. At the next stoplight, Brad lit his pipe and the two of them lapsed into a companionable silence. She didn't mention it to him, but she was thinking that she was glad he'd brought out his pipe. She found the mild, mellow odor of Brad's tobacco pleasing, and she relaxed against the car seat to enjoy the half-hour drive to the nearby lake.

The rain started again, and they drove the short distance over to Keystone and back in a continuous shower. Just before they arrived back at the Carlton Building, Brad let her know that he would be around Tulsa until the middle of the following week or longer. "There'll be lots of opportunities for business and pleasure. I intend to see that we engage in both." He smiled warmly and covered her hand with his, squeezing it in friendly intimacy.

If he had intended his statement to reassure her that the two of them would in time negotiate the lease between Carlton and El-Sa, it did not. Quite the opposite. Since he'd made it obvious that he was in no hurry to continue discussing business with her, and since he was planning on spending so much time in Tulsa, she wondered if that could mean that another oil company was also seeking to lease his mineral rights. She frowned, giving Brad an inquiring look. She felt uncertain how to handle things with him at this point, and she held off responding until they had reached the front of her building. "I'm counting on meeting and talking with you again the first of the week about those mineral rights, Brad,'' Claudia said, in what she hoped was a confident, businesslike tone.

''We'll talk before that.'' He drew the car close to the curb and leaned over to open the door for her, allowing his face to remain close to hers for an imperceptible instant before he moved aside to let her get out of the car. In that brief second she felt his magnetism so intensely she could almost believe he had actually kissed her.

Ducking her head, she made a dash for the building entrance. The downpour of rain pelted her head and shoulders, wetting her hair and soaking through the linenlike material of her suit jacket. Once inside the door she turned back, but Brad's copper-colored car had already disappeared around the corner.

Instead of leaving the elevator at the fourth floor to go to her own office, she rode on to the executive floor at the top of the building. She was curious about some of the things Brad had mentioned to her, and she wanted to talk to Myra a few minutes before she left.

Myra Allan's eyes widened with interest at the sight of Claudia. ''It's pouring down outside, I see. You obviously got caught out without your raincoat,'' she teased her boss's daughter good-naturedly.

''And without an umbrella,'' Claudia answered, fluffing water from the back of her hair as she walked nearer Myra's desk. ''It didn't seem to be coming down that heavy while we were driving, but when I was getting from the car into the building it was a deluge.'' Now she brushed anxiously at the sleeves of her jacket. ''I hope this suit doesn't spot or shrink.''

''Certainly is pretty on you.'' Myra indicated her entire outfit, skirt, blouse and jacket. ''You look like spring in that lovely jonquil yellow.''

"Ditto," Claudia told her, admiring the navy and white coat dress her father's secretary was wearing. Claudia had always thought Myra was pretty, although her features were far from perfect. Myra's nose was a trifle too long, her jaw too wide, and there was even a slightly stubborn line to her mouth, but it was these very irregularities that made hers a striking face with a look of cool, uncompromising honesty. She had very expressive eyes, amber with dark lashes and clearly arched dark brows. She wore her vibrant, glossy brown hair in a short, casual style that made her look neither younger nor older than her thirty-nine years.

Claudia now moved close enough to lean against the corner of Myra's desk. "I know it's almost five o'clock, but I hoped I could talk to you a few minutes before you leave. Are you in a hurry to get away?"

"Not in any great hurry. What's going on with you?" She folded her arms in front of her, giving Claudia an easy, relaxed smile. It was apparent that she liked Claudia and that the two of them had a good rapport with each other.

"I'm not sure just what to make of the strange kind of day this turned out to be. Since ten o'clock this morning I've been with this man from Texas, but I made little if any headway with him on the lease I want." She fingered the corner of the desk mindlessly. "Did you ever hear Dad mention El-Sa Corporation in Texas?"

Myra's thoughtful expression ended in a negative shake of her head. "I don't recall it. What's the location in Texas?"

"Abilene." Claudia paused, running the tip of her tongue across her upper lip, thinking about what Brad had said about his father. "Wait a minute," she said suddenly, putting both hands down flat on Myra's desk and angling her head forward. "Twenty years ago, when you first started working here, do you recall a man in the drilling business named Sam Hayes?"

Myra's shoulders stiffened slightly and she dropped her eyes, shielding them from Claudia's keen gaze. "I recall the name. Why?" Her tone was noncommittal, but she continued to keep her eyes averted.

"His son, Bradley Hayes, is the man I'm attempting to do business with. Brad is vice-president of El-Sa."

"That's—well, it's interesting in a way. Did you tell your father this?"

"I didn't know it before Dad left town. But Brad seems to think Dad and his father knew each other back then. Since you remember the name, then Brad was right. He said Sam Hayes would have been in and out of the office here back in those days."

"I know your dad will be interested in hearing about this. Tell him as soon as he gets back on Monday, won't you?" Myra was looking directly at Claudia, and she had raised her voice as if she wanted to stress to Claudia the importance of telling Howard about Sam Hayes and El-Sa Corporation. Myra hesitated as if she were going to add something further, but instead she looked at her watch and got up from her desk. "I'm sorry, Claudia, but I guess I'd better run. I'm going out to dinner and then to the Oilers ball game tonight, so I need to get home and change clothes."

Claudia arched an eyebrow, giving her father's secretary a knowing smile. "You going out with that lawyer friend who's been courting you for the past six months?" she asked.

"A dinner date and ball game every two or three weeks is hardly a courtship," Myra commented evenly.

"It could be if you'd let it. This man is obviously

interested in you. Don't tell me you're never going to think about getting married again?''

A rosy flush spread across Myra's cheeks, causing Claudia to wish that she hadn't been so outspoken. She knew, of course, that Myra's husband had been killed in Vietnam. But that had been long years ago. She was surprised that Myra hadn't married again before this.

The attractive, brown-haired woman put one hand to her face to mask the heightened color in her cheeks. ''I think about it,'' she said in a tight voice. ''It's just that the right man hasn't asked me.'' She rubbed the side of her face, then moved her hand lower and covered her neck. Her movements revealed how ill at ease she had become.

A curious look clouded Claudia's eyes as the full import of what Myra had said occurred to her. She hadn't said she hadn't found the right man, the one she wanted to marry. She'd said the right man hadn't asked her. Claudia chewed her bottom lip thoughtfully. Now exactly what did that mean? she wondered. More to the point, who might the right man for Myra be?

Chapter Three

Claudia wakened early the following morning, pleased to discover that the cool air of the spring dawn gave signs of melting into sudden warmth. The sun had already licked away all the traces of yesterday's rain, and the sky was as blue as a robin's egg and cloudless.

Since Saturday morning was the time she kept for cleaning her apartment every week, she dressed in faded jeans, a bandanna print shirt and a pair of sneakers. After quickly stripping the sheets off her bed, she started the washing machine and put in the dirty laundry as she sipped on a tall glass of orange juice. With her chores started, she sat down at the counter bar in her small kitchen long enough to eat a bowl of corn flakes and drink a cup of instant coffee.

Claudia's apartment was of moderate size and well designed to give it the look and feel of space and openness. No walls divided the living room from the small dining room or the kitchen. The kitchen was visually separated from the living room, however, by a U-shaped counter that wrapped almost all the way around the perimeter. Claudia had painstakingly decorated the apartment throughout in her favorite colors of blue and yellow, so it both pleased and suited her.

Having no special plans for later in the day, she took her time with her housecleaning, spending almost an hour polishing her collection of antique brass candlesticks and then rearranging them symmetrically at one end of the mantel above her fireplace. The final order of the morning was the winding of the hundred-year-old Seth Thomas clock, which sat on the other end of the mantel from the brass candlesticks. Made of black ebony, the clock was Claudia's treasure, and she'd been delighted when her mother gave it to her at the time the family home was sold. As a child, Claudia had been fascinated by the rhythmic ticking of the old eight-day clock, and she still loved the noisy bonging sound it made striking each hour. The sounds it made were familiar, companionable. There were times when it seemed to dispel feelings of loneliness for her.

Her clock began to strike loudly twelve times in rapid succession while Claudia was storing the vacuum cleaner back in the utility closet next to the clothes washer and dryer. Deciding she would get her shower and wash her hair before taking time to have lunch, she pulled off her shirt and jeans and headed for the bathroom. As she was stepping into the shower the phone started to ring.

At first she decided to ignore it, but the next second she remembered that she didn't have a date for the evening and thought how nice it would be if someone was calling to ask her out. Up until a few weeks ago she had been going with an entertaining fellow who was in Tulsa on a training and indoctrination program with a major oil company, but he had been assigned to the Houston office and had moved to Texas. The shrill jangle continued persistently. Snatching her robe, Claudia ran barefoot back into the bedroom and grabbed up the telephone as it rang for the sixth time.

"Hello," she said breathlessly.

"I was about to give you up, but I did tell you Capricorns are persistent, remember?" Brad's deep voice had a good-natured sound. "You sound as if you just came in from jogging. Did you?"

"No. I was getting into the shower," she explained. "I just spent the morning giving my apartment a good cleanup."

"Good. Then you've finished all your chores and there's nothing to keep you from going sailing with me this afternoon."

Claudia smiled, liking his suggestion. "Nothing if you have a sailboat," she teased him, adding, "I don't recall seeing one strapped to the top of your car yesterday when we drove to Lake Keystone."

"You get feisty when the sun shines, don't you?" he chided her. "And yes, I do have a boat. I have the use of my friend's Snipe, and it'll handle well on a day like this. The wind is just right, brisk enough to give us a fine sail. So get ready and I'll pick you up in an hour." His exuberance was infectious.

"Make that two hours and pick me up at the Ford garage downtown. I need to leave my car there for service."

As she hung up the phone and headed back for her shower, she realized she was smiling broadly. Brad had sounded really enthusiastic about having her sail with him. She liked that. In fact she liked him, and she felt excited

about being with him again. It was lucky that the rain had
ended the night before so that the day was clear and sunny
and with a brisk wind just right for a sail. She laughed
aloud at this thought as she stepped into the shower. It
appeared nature had conspired for her this day, and she
was duly grateful.

When they arrived at the marina, Brad pointed to a slip
that held a small boat with a colorful blue and white
striped mainsail and a white jib. ''You match the sails,''
he said, with an admiring glance at her white slacks and
bright blue T-shirt. ''And that's not all you and this boat
have in common.'' He cupped her shoulders, his merry
brown eyes smiling down into hers. ''You're both beautiful and a joy to handle.'' Brad moved his hands slowly
down the length of her arms, catching her hands warmly
in his. It was absurd how his touch excited her.

''I think for this afternoon you had best stick to
handling just the boat. What if I handle the jib sheets when
we're tacking, and you take the mainsail and the tiller.''

''Well, well.'' Brad's lower lip shot out and he pressed
her hands more firmly in his. ''You know something about
sailing, don't you?''

''Maybe as much as you do.'' She wrinkled her nose
provocatively. ''My mother loved sailing and it became
the one thing we did as a family. She kept at Dad until he
bought a place on Grand Lake O' the Cherokees, and at
one time we even had two sailboats. From the time I was
twelve until I was about fifteen we spent a lot of weekends
up there. It was the happiest time we ever had.'' Her face
sobered, and the sparkle vanished from her blue eyes.
''My parents divorced during my first year in college,''
she added with a shrug. ''So I associate sailing with that
earlier, better time. My nicest memories of my mother go

with it.'' She drew in her breath sharply, aware suddenly of saying much more than she had ever intended. What on earth had prompted her to go on so about her mother?

Brad let go of her hands, immediately circling her waist with his arm. They walked together down the dock and came alongside the boat with the blue and white sail. ''I'm darn glad you were brought up to like sailing, Claudia,'' Brad said, hugging her snugly against his side. ''Like mother, like daughter, right?''

She flinched as if he'd struck her, jerking free of the arm holding her waist. ''Don't say that. It's a stupid cliché and I hate clichés.'' The words exploded shrilly out of her mouth. ''I'm not like my mother. Not at all. A daughter doesn't have to be like her mother any more than a son has to be a 'chip off the old block.' And that is another one of those dreadful old clichés.'' Claudia could feel herself trembling all over now, but she kept on pouring out words as if she couldn't stop. ''I don't want to be like my mother, and I won't let myself be. I'm a different person from her, from anybody. I'm me, and so the only one I'm like is just me.'' Her voice cracked in a harsh splintering sound that was almost a sob.

''Hey now,'' he said gently, puzzled concern lining his face. ''I mouthed a trite saying, but I never thought I was saying anything to upset you. I'm sorry if I did.''

Claudia swallowed hard, trying to get a hold on her emotions. She'd made a fool of herself with her defiant outburst. Brad didn't really know her and he'd never known Vanessa. There was no way he could understand why she would flare out at him so. She'd never revealed her feelings to anyone before, and she shouldn't have now.

Brad still scrutinized her face, searching for an explanation of her dramatic reaction to his lightly spoken words.

After a long moment of silence between them he said, "Let's take the boat out now, Claudia. Give me your hand; I'll help you aboard." He extended his arm, reaching out to her.

She put her hand in his and he curled his fingers firmly around hers. Her fingers felt cold, and they still trembled in the emotional aftermath. His hand warmed hers instantly, easing her anxieties as if by magic. The tense line of her mouth softened, gentling the fullness of her lips. A caressing smile was beginning to seep into Brad's sensual eyes.

Gently but insistently he pulled her into his arms. Then he slowly lowered his head and his lips touched hers in a warm and tender caress. He held her lightly at first, then pressed her firmly to him.

As if propelled by an unknown force, she put her arms around his neck. As the pressure of his lips increased, she responded hesitantly at first and then with much less restraint. She was filled with an unfamiliar and strangely exciting warmth. A confused mixture of thoughts whirled around in the far recesses of her mind. What was happening to her? Why was Brad doing this? An open dock at a public marina was hardly the setting for their continuing embrace. She moved her face away, burying it for a moment against the strong wall of his chest. For a while they just stood there, not saying anything, Brad's arms remaining firmly around her. After a few minutes he eased his hold of her but did not let her go.

"We do this very well together, you know that?" he said softly, his words muffled because his lips were now pressed into the soft, silky hair curled over her temples. "I think we ought to try it once more."

"And I think it would be better if we got on the boat.

We did come here to sail, remember!'' She eased herself free of his embrace and stepped back away from him. She lowered her eyes, not wanting him to see the effect his nearness was having on her.

"Can I help it if I discovered something better for us to do?'' He reached over and put his hand under her chin, forcing her to lift her face and look at him.

Gathering the remnants of her senses, she smiled. ''Oh, I thought that was my reward for having sailing skills.'' She spun away from him, jumping quickly from the dock onto the deck of the small sailboat.

Brad followed her, leaping aboard with catlike grace. ''I know better than to comment on that statement, Claudia. But I am discovering that you have a number of exciting skills.'' Laughing, he cast off the bow and stern lines and pushed the boom out so the wind would catch the sails.

For the next two hours they tacked back and forth across the blue-green water of Lake Keystone. The breeze was gentle, but it blew enough to cause small wavelets on the surface of the water. Along the shore the light wind visibly stirred the leafy branches of the trees. Toward the end of the day the wind picked up. To cut down on the spray, Brad lowered the mainsail, tied down the reef points and then hauled the sail taut. They continued sailing for another forty-five minutes before heading in. Claudia first took in the jib; then together she and Brad doused the mainsail before reaching the dock.

"Tired?'' Brad asked, as they got back in Brad's car to drive away from the marina.

"Not tired as much as windblown.'' She pushed her sunglasses up above her forehead, letting them rest in the wind-rumpled hair atop her head. Gently she laid her palms against the sides of her face, feeling the heat in her rosy cheeks. "Am I sunburned? My face feels mighty warm."

Brad glanced over at her and shook his head. "You have a healthy glow that's very becoming, but that's all." Reaching up, he drew her left hand away from her face and, lacing his fingers together with hers, he held her hand, resting it on the seat between them.

They drove along in companionable silence. "Where are we going?" she asked after they'd driven a short distance away from the marina.

"Someplace to have dinner where we'll be okay as we are, dressed in our sailing clothes, if that suits you."

"It sure does. I didn't have time for much lunch, and now I'm hungry enough to eat a bear."

"I doubt if I can get you bear here in Oklahoma," he said with a straight face, but his eyes twinkled with humor. "I do know of a plain, simple restaurant near here that's rumored to have the best fried catfish in the state, however. Will you settle for fish instead of bear?"

Claudia's enthusiastic nod was all the answer Brad needed.

As they drove up to the restaurant, Claudia thought it looked like a typical truck stop cafe; there was even a sixteen-wheeler parked near the side of the cement block building. Inside, however, she discovered the place was larger than she'd thought. Instead of just one room there were two rather large rooms decorated in various shades of green, the color of trees and plants, restful but cheerful at the same time.

The tables and matching chairs were of natural oak, lightly stained and varnished to give them an attractive finish. Each table was covered with a bright green cloth.

"I like this place. It's not so plain; in fact, it's attractive," Claudia whispered under her breath to Brad as they walked through to the back room and took a table against the side wall.

"It's like a darn forest," he whispered back to her. "Guess what the cook's favorite color is. Also the owner's and the owner's wife's." They sat down, and almost instantly a young girl in green slacks and a white blouse set green water glasses in front of them. Brad and Claudia exchanged glances and both began to laugh. Brad slid his hand across the top of the table until his fingertips were touching hers. They continued to laugh intimately in unspoken acknowledgment that they had shared the same thought at the same time, adding a new dimension of closeness between them.

Brad's expression changed, becoming faintly quizzical. "It's impossible that I've only known you a couple of days. At this moment I feel I must have known you all your life."

Claudia's laughter evaporated as abruptly as Brad's. It was as if she sensed exactly what he did, and she was acutely aware that there was a chemistry between them that bound them together profoundly. For an endless moment his eyes held hers as the seriousness of their emotions enveloped them completely.

"How old are you, Claudia?" Brad asked finally, breaking the intimate silence between them.

She felt dazed, and she couldn't distinguish his words for the rushing sensation that filled her ears. "Wh-what?"

"How old are you?" he repeated with a disarming smile. "If part of my being has always been aware of your existence, I want to know for how many years that's been."

"How long do you think?" she managed to counter lightly, feigning a composure she was far from feeling.

"When did you get your engineering degree?"

"Last May, almost a year ago now."

"Then I think you must be twenty-two. Am I right?"

She nodded affirmatively. "And you're twenty-nine. So you can't make me believe you would have bothered to know a scrawny little towheaded girl who was seven years younger than you were."

"I'm certainly bothering now." He moved his hand until it covered hers. "And I can assure you that she's no longer scrawny, and her towhead is now the rich gold color of summer wheat."

Brad kept his hand pressed warmly over hers. Neither of them moved. Claudia could feel the electricity vibrating between them. What was the powerful attraction Brad held for her? How could she feel something deep and special and exciting, and at the same time be afraid? And was it Brad she was afraid of or was it herself? There were stirrings deep inside her, feelings and emotions that she couldn't suppress. And she didn't want to. Did that mean she was like her mother? She lowered her head, concentrating her gaze on the dark green glass of the water tumbler on the table in front of her. A few seconds later Brad took his hand from hers. She felt a stab of regret that he was no longer touching her and that they were no longer linked together in a tangible way.

The cafe had appeared fairly well filled when they first arrived, but by the time the pretty waitress came back to take their order, several more people had come in. The back room now had every table filled except for one. Eating spots in Oklahoma's lake areas always drew a crowd on a Saturday night, but Claudia imagined the restaurant's reputation for well-cooked catfish accounted for its extra popularity. Because of the number to be served, it took quite a while to get their dinner, but it was worth the wait. After eating every bite of her dinner, Claudia joined Brad in eating fresh-baked apple pie accompanied by large cups of rich black coffee. It seemed the later it became, the noisier the cafe crowd became. It was a relief to leave and enjoy the quiet of the night as they walked back to their car.

It was a clear night with a lopsided moon shedding its butter yellow light into the dark blue heaven. The scattering of stars that attended the moon appeared like a handful of silver sequins tossed into the night sky.

Brad swung the car back onto the wide highway, and in a surprisingly brief time, it seemed, Claudia caught sight of the magnificent Tulsa skyline with the glowing lights of towering buildings adding their touch of splendor to the clear night sky. Viewed in the daylight, the slender shafts were merely tall buildings; at night, with their lighted towers, they became beacons depicting the vibrant, aggressive spirit of Tulsa. This was a sight she loved.

Though she wasn't conscious of doing it, Claudia must have made an audible sigh, for Brad turned to her. "Was that a sigh or a yawn? Are you happy or sleepy?" he asked in a low, quiet voice.

"Happy, and I guess awestruck by the sight of Tulsa at night." She touched his arm as if to insure his attention. "It's incredibly beautiful, isn't it? Don't tell me you can beat it, even in Texas."

He glanced at her and smiled. "Don't worry, I won't. I feel just like you do. I'm a native Tulsan, after all. I just had the bad luck to be uprooted."

Claudia studied his face in the dim light of the car's

interior. Though he had smiled, she thought she detected a hint of sadness in his face and even anger in his voice when he spoke of being uprooted. She patted his arm, somehow wanting to comfort him. "How old were you when your family moved away from Tulsa?"

"Eleven, nearly twelve." He paused thoughtfully, and at the same time he slowed the car's speed slightly. "No one can ever know just how much I hated to leave Tulsa. I was born here and I wanted to stay. I resented having to leave my school, my friends, the nice big house I'd always lived in."

There was an unmistakable edge to his voice now, and though he hadn't moved his arm, Claudia definitely sensed his withdrawal from her. Taking her hand from his arm, she laced her fingers together, pressing her hands firmly in her lap. "Brad, you told me that your father started his first drilling company here. Why did he want to leave?"

"It wasn't what he wanted; it was what someone else seemed to want. Actually was determined to have. A man my father considered to be his friend set out to ruin Dad's business, and he accomplished that and more. My family lost more than money. There were personal losses, physical ones. My mother as well as my father were harmed. Damn!" he exploded, then stopped abruptly, suddenly accelerating the car. "It's nothing you'd care to hear about. Let's drop it."

She stared at his profile, the grim set of his jaw, the anger-etched lines that marked the corners of his eyes. She wanted to apologize for asking upsetting questions, but she didn't want to embarrass him or anger him further. Realizing she was still studying him, she turned her head, looking through the windshield at the taillights of the car ahead. She didn't talk again until they were driving through the south part of Tulsa on Skelly Drive. Then she told him which exit to take and gave directions for reaching her apartment.

"This looks like a fairly new complex. How long have you lived here?" Brad asked as they left the car and walked slowly to the door of her apartment.

"I moved in last July. The apartments weren't all completed then, but I chose the one I wanted and got to choose my wall color, carpets and drapes. I'm lucky because I have my apartment decorated in my favorite color."

"Please tell me it's not green," he said in a pained voice.

Claudia laughed. "No, it's not green." As they reached her door, she opened her purse and felt around inside for her keys.

"I really didn't think it was." He waited while she located her door key and then put it in the lock. "I'd say your favorite color is blue."

She flipped her head up at him, a look of pleased surprise on her face. "You're right. That was a lucky guess."

"No, a calculated one."

If he was trying to mystify and intrigue her, he was succeeding. She pursed her lips thoughtfully. "Calculated? Okay, how and based on what facts?"

"Let me inside to say good night and I'll tell you."

Claudia's eyes wrinkled at the corners in a knowing smile. "Now I get it. This is a line you use to get into a girl's apartment. Tell me, does it usually work?"

"I don't know. This is the first time I've tried it."

Shrugging, she stepped aside so he could turn her key

in the lock and open the door for her. "I don't believe you. I think you're quite accustomed to getting anything you want. But you have me curious. I want to find out how you came to your conclusion that my color is blue." She smiled and preceded him through the door.

She'd left one light on in the living room when she'd gone out at noon because she hated to come home to a dark apartment. Now she turned on another and laid her purse down on the lamp table next to the antique velvet sofa of azure blue. "Look around if you like," she said, walking toward the kitchen. "I'll fix us something to drink if you can go for instant tea or coffee. I'm afraid that's all I've got."

"I'd like iced tea, if it's no trouble." Brad stood in the middle of the room for a few minutes, letting his gaze take in the furnishings and the interesting groupings of pictures Claudia had hung to decorate her walls. After a cursory look he walked over to the fireplace and began to examine the things on the mantel. "I see you like brass," he called to her.

"I like candlesticks mostly." Her words were accompanied by the clinking of ice against glass as she dropped in ice cubes and then stirred the instant tea mixture vigorously.

"Are you an ardent collector?"

Claudia came from the kitchen carrying their iced tea on a tray with sugar and a little squirt bottle of lemon juice. She set it down on the coffee table in front of the sofa before walking over to join Brad by the mantel. "I guess I could be, except I don't have much more room left on the mantel." She laughed, reaching up to push two of the candlesticks a bit closer together.

Brad placed his strong hands on either side of Claudia's

waist, pulling her away from the mantel and bringing her into his arms. Wordlessly, he looked at her, his eyes deep, dark and glowing. She felt almost hypnotized by the penetrating warmth of his lustrous brown eyes. A sensuous heat flowed through her, wonderful, thrilling and frightening all at once.

Claudia watched his face moving closer. Then she felt his lips as they closed over hers, causing a sweet thrill of excitement to quiver down her spine. She trembled with the sudden knowledge that she couldn't play it cool with a man like Brad. His charming appeal was as potent as warm brandy, its effect inevitable.

Brad's arms held her lightly against him, his lips moving gently over hers, teasing her into response. As his arms gradually tightened around her, the touch of his lips grew firmer, his kiss more intimate. Claudia abandoned all reserve—she couldn't do anything else, didn't want to do anything else. She put her arms around him and held him, her fingers spread and each one pressing firmly against his broad back. She touched him without restraint because it was good and natural and the only way she was capable of responding.

When finally they drew apart, Claudia was aware of a faint embarrassment at her own lack of restraint. "We're letting the ice melt in our iced tea," she murmured inanely, a flush spreading over her throat and edging into her face.

"I think we've melted more than ice," Brad said, his voice low and a little husky.

She lowered her eyes and took a step away from him. "We were going to discuss how you calculated that my favorite color is blue," she said, changing the subject abruptly. "That's why you came in to see my apartment, remember?'' She walked over to the coffee table and picked up one of the glasses of tea, put a few drops of lemon juice in it and then carried it over to the sofa and sat down.

Brad watched her, a smile tugging at the corners of his lips. Following her lead, he took the remaining glass from the tray and walked over to sit in an ivory and blue upholstered chair opposite the sofa. Frowning, he immediately leaned forward to remove a small round pillow from behind his back. ''You may have an interior decorator that insisted on this, but throw pillows gall me.'' He tossed it playfully at her, but aimed it so it would land on the floor at her feet and not in her lap.

''Sorry,'' she laughed. ''It's another of my blue touches. More for looks than to give comfort. Now that you're settled with your tea, explain about your lucky guess.''

''My discerning evaluation based on astute observations,'' he corrected her.

''Whatever.'' She grimaced and took a drink of her tea.

''Well, it really wasn't the most difficult thing I ever figured out. Like I said, there were a number of clues and all of them blue. First of all, you were wearing blue the first afternoon when you came to the well site, and you're wearing blue again today. Obviously it's a color you like to wear—and incidentally, you should always wear something blue. It becomes you and goes with those incredibly pretty eyes of yours.'' He paused, taking the time to look deeply into those eyes.

Brad's compliment more than just pleased her. A feeling of warm elation spread all through her. He remembered the cornflower blue skirt and blouse she'd worn the first time he'd seen her. Obviously he'd been more aware of her that afternoon than she would ever have imagined. Realizing it made her feel deliciously smug, and she smiled inwardly at her own vanity.

If Brad guessed what she was thinking, he didn't let on but continued with his explanation. "Also, of course, there's the fact that you drive a car with a metallic blue paint job." He propped one elbow on the arm of his chair and waited for her to comment.

She looked at him over the rim of her glass as she continued drinking her tea. "That's all? You expect me to believe you figured out my color because of my clothes and my car?" She shook her head at him, teasing him with a skeptical arch of her brows.

Brad got up and walked over to the sofa, set his glass down on the coffee table, then sat down beside Claudia. "You win," he said, chuckling under his breath. "It was a lucky guess." His eyes were full of laughing lights as he took her tea away from her and set her glass on the table next to his. He kept hold of her hand, running his thumb across her long graceful fingers, caressing them. "I think we've settled that point, and now I want to discover more about you than just your favorite color."

Her heart quickened. His words were like an intimate touch, sensuous and suggestive. She felt herself trembling.

Brad moved his hands along her arms; then, taking hold of her shoulders, he gently but insistently pushed her down into the blue velvet cushions of the sofa.

Involuntarily she closed her eyes for a second. When she opened them Brad's handsome face was just a breath away from her own. His eyes held hers, and she stared back at him, returning his passionate gaze.

"I bet you didn't know that your eyes change from blue

to silvery gray in the most intriguing and beautiful way. I think they mirror your emotions, and I must find out which emotions make them blue and which gray.'' There was no levity in his words. His tone and expression were wholly serious. His fingers played with the soft curls that edged her face, then moved slowly over her cheek and down to touch her lips. His eyes held hers as his hand traveled down her chin and throat, continuing until his hand covered her breast.

Claudia could feel warm color surge into her cheeks as he gently caressed her. Brad's eyes grew dark with desire, and he slowly put his mouth down on hers. Every fiber of Claudia's being came to life as the warmth of his lips met hers, first gently, then with a more insistent demand as the kiss grew. She was drawn to him inexorably, with an insatiable need for his touch and a sudden hungry longing she had never experienced before with any other man.

Oh, my God! What was she doing? She was no different from her mother! Moving her mouth from his, she buried her face in his shoulder.

''Don't hide from me,'' Brad murmured, resting his lips against her hair. ''I want to hold you and kiss you. More than that, I want to—''

''Please,'' she stopped him, anguish sounding in her voice. ''Don't say anything more to me.''

Brad pressed her close against his chest and just held her quietly for several minutes before pulling her into a sitting position and releasing her slowly. ''I know that in sailing, running before the wind puts the boat's balance in jeopardy and can even sometimes cause the boat to capsize. I've no intention of running before the wind with you, Claudia,'' he said softly.

For a fraction of a moment he laid the palm of his hand

against the side of her face. Then he got to his feet, strode across the room and let himself out the door.

Claudia heard the door click shut after Brad, and at the same time the old clock on the mantel began its noisy bonging of the hour. It struck twelve times. The reverberating sound was loud, echoing harshly through the room where Claudia now sat alone.

Chapter Four

As the twelfth tone of the clock's striking faded completely away, Claudia had an absurd, even funny thought occur
to her. At the stroke of midnight Cinderella had been
forced to face her own reality and flee from her Prince
Charming, a prince she'd fallen in love with in just one
night. Was it possible that she had fallen in love with Brad
after knowing him only these few days? Brad had said that
he felt as if he'd known her always. That was a romantic
thing to say, compellingly exciting, but emotional rather
than factual.

Claudia ran her hands through the sides of her hair, then
began to massage her temples with a gentle, circular
motion of her fingertips, hoping this would stimulate her
brain to think rationally. But was it possible to be rational
about what seemed to be happening to her? she wondered.

She recalled that moment in the restaurant when she had
felt such an overpowering emotion for Brad. At that

moment he had only been touching her fingertips with his and looking at her across that vivid green tablecloth. If she put a name to this emotion, would she call it love?

Leaning over, she picked up the round blue pillow that Brad had tossed over at her feet. She hugged it to her breast, letting her chin touch the corded edge of the silky fabric covering. And what was she feeling now with the warm imprint of his kiss and the caress of his touch vivid in her memory? Love, she was feeling love. For the first time in her life she loved a man with the most honest of passionate emotions, and it was glorious and frightening at the same time.

She got unsteadily to her feet, and without being aware of doing it, she placed the blue pillow back in the ivory-colored chair and walked over to study her reflection in the wide mirror that extended from the top of the dado to the ceiling, forming one wall of the dining room. She saw that her blue eyes were luminous, glowing with a silver sheen. She wondered if the emotion they now mirrored was the same one Brad had seen.

Claudia knew that she would not be seeing Brad again until Monday afternoon, when he'd be at her office to talk about the Stephens County lease. She'd set the time as late as possible, hoping against hope that her father would get back in Tulsa in time for her to talk with him before meeting with Brad.

She asked Myra to tell Howard that she had to see him immediately when he got back to the office. So at a quarter after one on Monday afternoon Claudia was walking into her father's office, the El-Sa file clutched determinedly in her hand.

"Dad, I'm so darn glad you're back."

At the sight of his daughter marching rapidly through

the door of his office, Howard stood up and came from behind his desk to greet her. "That's the most enthusiastic welcome I've had in a long time, and I appreciate it." He smiled warmly, hugging her around the shoulders and then kissing her lightly on the forehead, as he had done since she was a little girl, claiming then that it was the only area of her face not bearing sticky traces of peanut butter and jelly. "And incidentally, another thing I appreciate is how perfectly you took care of the flowers for Myra. She was enormously pleased and amazed that I remembered that she liked pink carnations." Howard gave Claudia a conspiratorial wink. "Did you see them outside on her desk?"

Claudia shook her head. "I was in too much of a hurry. I'll see them later." She clipped her words, revealing the nervous tension she was feeling. "Right now, Dad, I need your advice and I've got some questions I need answered," she said tersely. "There's not much time because I've got this appointment at three about the lease we want in Stephens County." She waved her hand, indicating she wanted him to sit back down at his desk, and at the same time she pulled a russet leather side chair up next to her father's desk and sat down. "When I get the lease on this area, the company will have all we need in order to start drilling."

Howard leaned back in his chair, clasping his hands behind his head, a pleased look on his face. He was obviously proud of his daughter, and his words echoed the look of pride in his eyes as he studied her pretty face. "You've moved right along on this whole project if you've already acquired the mineral rights on everything we need except for just one piece. Who has it?"

"El-Sa. It's a Texas corporation."

"I don't think I know of El-Sa. Is it in Houston or Dallas?" He swiveled his chair idly in a relaxed manner.

"Neither one. It's in Abilene. Actually it's a family corporation involving two companies, Hayes Oil Field Supply and Alamo Drilling Company."

Howard jerked forward, straightening rigidly in his chair. "Sam Hayes *is* Alamo Drilling. By God, Claudia! Don't tell me you've been in contact with Sam Hayes?"

She stared openmouthed at her father, amazed at his volatile reaction to the mention of Alamo Drilling Company and Brad's father. "The man I'm seeing is the son, Brad Hayes. He's vice-president of El-Sa."

"Well, you can forget about it. If Sam Hayes is connected with it, there'll be no deal made with Carlton. Why, this son of his won't even listen to our offer much less get into discussing terms. You can take my word for it." He held his chin between his thumb and index finger, scowling darkly.

"I think you're wrong. Brad and I met and talked about it Friday. I also spent most of the day Saturday with him. He's a smart, fairly agreeable fellow to do business with. Now, I'm not saying there aren't a number of things that will have to be ironed out, but I feel if you allow me to go up on the amount of the lease bonus there's a good chance I can get him to agree to the lease. Brad does want a lot more money than we offered. And he insists on one stipulation: that any drilling on his lease must be contracted to Alamo Drilling. But he agreed that they'd meet any other company's bid for the job."

Howard slapped his hands down on the arms of his chair. "I don't buy a word of it," he said, shaking his slightly graying dark head. "Sam Hayes will never again set one of his drilling rigs on a piece of land that I have any part of. I know that for a fact. The man hates me, Claudia. I can't say I altogether blame him.''

"You believe a man hates you and then you say you don't blame him. I don't understand this. I want you to explain to me what you're talking about.''

Howard's face knotted in a pained expression. The deep lines that grooved his eyes at that moment made him appear tired and older than his forty-nine years. "It's unpleasant and nothing I want to talk about. Besides, you don't need to know and I'd rather you didn't.''

"Dad, for heaven's sake.'' Claudia's voice rose in frustration as well as irritation. "How can I deal intelligently with Brad on this if I don't know what the problem is that exists between our company and his, and between you and his father?''

"I'll tell you this. My family and this company have been the most important things in my life. And right or wrong, I've done whatever I felt I had to do in order to preserve both. Ending my verbal agreement with Sam Hayes eighteen years ago was one of the things I thought I had to do to save what was mine.''

She looked at her father aghast. "Surely you're not saying you reneged on a verbal contract?''

" 'Ended' is a better word. I ended a working agreement that I had with a friend. At the time I felt I had strong cause for what I did.'' Howard gripped the arms of his desk chair, pushing himself up from the seat to stand behind his desk. "Sam and I had a satisfactory arrangement in the beginning. One that was highly profitable to us both. His company drilled every Carlton well exclusively, and in return he gave us a low competitive price.''

"Then why did you want to end it?''

Howard frowned, crossing his arms across his chest. "For a number of reasons, Claudia. All of which seemed valid to me at the time. Now let's not talk anymore about me and Sam Hayes,'' he said, a note of finality in his voice. He walked to the large window behind his desk, standing before it looking out, his back to Claudia.

Claudia gritted her teeth and clamped her lips firmly together. It would do no good to argue with her father or try to question him further. She knew only too well that when Howard Carlton said a subject was closed, it was just that. She pushed her own chair back and stood up, but she didn't follow her father over to the window. Instead, she took a step toward the door to indicate she felt she needed to leave. "Dad, I've got to be getting down to my office, but I'm begging you not to tie my hands on this lease with El-Sa. You know this is important for the company, and I'm confident I can get Brad to sign a lease if you'll authorize a higher offer.''

"We've made a fair and realistic offer now,'' he answered her with his back still toward her. "How much more does this young Hayes want?''

"Twice as much,'' she said in an even but quiet voice as if anticipating her father's reaction.

Howard turned around sharply. "That's not only exorbitant, it's absurd. If he asked that much, it's Sam's doing. He intends to gouge us on this to get a measure of revenge on me.''

"You're right, of course. Twice the amount we've offered is out of the question. But Dad, we are talking about proven acreage. Let me go as high as half again on the lease bonus. Will you okay that?''

He rammed one hand into his pocket, his eyes narrowed and thoughtful. After a tense moment of silence between them he nodded his head.

Claudia wasn't going to give him a chance to change his mind. "Thanks. I'll handle it from here.'' She tossed her words at him, and with a confident smile on her face she rushed out the door of his office.

Brad was late. When he hadn't arrived at her office by three-thirty, Claudia could feel the tension welling up inside her. Too unsettled to stay seated at her desk, she moved over to stand before the tall plant placed decoratively in front of the plate glass window. Mindlessly, she fingered the spreading leaves. What was she so nervous about? She knew Brad had a good deal of other business to attend to in Tulsa. He had probably been detained somewhere. But if he had, why didn't he telephone? Tell her what time she could expect to see him? Realizing she was pulling at the edges of the green leaves, she thrust both of her hands into the slant pockets of her navy linen skirt and stared unseeingly out the window.

She heard his footsteps a second before Brad said her name. She spun around in time to see him striding through the door of her small office.

"I'm late and I'm sorry," he said tersely, then softened his blunt words with an apologetic smile. "I got tied up after lunch and had difficulty breaking away." He crossed the space that separated them and stood beside her in front of the window. "How was your day?" His tone remained conversational, but his eyes appraised her warmly.

"Pretty good. Yours?"

"Merely so-so. It's much better now that I'm seeing you."

"That's a nice thing to say, besides being charming and making it impossible for me to be angry at you for being late."

"I didn't say it for that reason," he answered in a low tone, letting his eyes linger on her face. "It's the truth.

The best part of this day for me will be whatever time I can spend with you.''

The awkwardness she'd felt with him when he first came in had now eased. ''Brad, please, it's time for us to talk about those mineral rights your corporation holds.'' She started toward her desk, then waited to sit down until he'd pulled up a chair facing hers. ''The way I see it, we're already in accord on most of the terms of the lease. We have no problem with using Alamo rigs for the drilling on that lease. I've cleared all of that. Now we need to agree on the amount of the lease bonus.'' She paused, glancing at him to decide what her tactic should be. ''We've offered a thousand dollars an acre and you want double that.'' She stated the fact in a careful, businesslike tone. At the same time she reached for a pencil and took time to jot figures on a scratch pad she had on her desk before she said anything more.

Brad observed her silently. He appeared totally willing to let her do all the talking, at least to start with. When she reached for her pencil, he had casually drawn his pipe out of his pocket. Now he methodically pressed tobacco into the bowl. ''You don't mind if I smoke this, do you?''

Shaking her head, she tapped the eraser end of the pencil against the palm of one hand. ''Two thousand dollars an acre is completely unrealistic for that tract. Now be honest, Brad, and admit it.''

He struck a match and lit his pipe. ''That's El-Sa's figure,'' he said, his chin at a stubborn angle. ''You and I both know about the well a mile away from this acreage that's now making eight hundred barrels a day.''

''Our company considered that, and that's why we went as high as we did at the start with you.'' She tapped the pencil a bit harder against the center of her hand. ''I'll tell you what. No other oil company would go even as high as twelve hundred and fifty, and I know darn well you're aware of that. Carlton will give you fifteen hundred an acre, but that's absolute top." Inclining her head toward him, she curved her lips in a faint smile. "Let's do business on that basis, Brad."

Removing his pipe from his mouth, he pushed a stream of smoke through his lips. "It's not entirely my decision, Claudia."

"I know, but talk it over with El-Sa. Take the time that you need. I'm willing to wait for the right answer," she added, smiling.

"I'll take your offer back to Abilene when I go tomorrow."

"Tomorrow," she echoed in surprise. "I thought you were going to be in Tulsa all this week."

"That was my first plan, but I ran into a delay with some of my arrangements. I can't accomplish what I intended for another week, so I'll go back to Abilene and return here sometime the end of next week."

Before Claudia could question him further about his plans, her phone rang.

"Claudia, I hope Brad Hayes is still in your office. Is he?" her father's brisk, decisive voice questioned her.

"Yes. As a matter of fact . . . yes," she came back at him, a rising inflection in her voice.

"Good. Then this is what I want you to do. See if he can have lunch with you and me tomorrow at the Tulsa Club. I've decided it's important that I meet Sam's son."

"I'm afraid tomorrow is out. He won't be in Tulsa after tonight." Claudia glanced at Brad as she spoke, wondering if he guessed she was talking about him. If he did, he didn't let on. He sat relaxed in his chair, smoking his pipe.

"Set it up for dinner tonight then."

"All right, I'll see what I can do and get back to you shortly," she assured him quickly, and hung up the phone. Looking at Brad, she fingered the collar of her white silk blouse. Why did her father have this sudden interest in meeting Brad Hayes? she wondered. "That was my father. He wanted me to ask you to have dinner at the Tulsa Club with us tonight."

Brad's relaxed manner changed and the lines tightened on his face. "I thought you told me he was out of town."

"Well, yes—yes I did, but he returned this morning."

"Then you told him about me, our business together?"

"Well, of course I did." She shrugged and gave a little laugh. "I talked to him just before you came this afternoon, to get his okay to raise the offer for the lease."

"I see," he muttered, but he continued to frown and his eyes were narrowed curiously.

She would have thought Brad would be pleased by her father's invitation to dinner. But apparently he wasn't. She was finding Brad's attitude a little irritating. "I'm sorry if you already have plans for tonight. Dad mentioned lunch tomorrow, but of course you'll be on your way back to Abilene. He had hoped to meet the vice-president of El-Sa and Sam Hayes's son," she said with cool matter-of-factness.

A vivid flicker of emotion marked Brad's eyes and darted across his face, accompanied by a twitch of the nerve in one cheek.

"I'm eager to meet him as well." Brad leaned over in order to empty the burned tobacco from his pipe into a clear glass ashtray on Claudia's desk. "And I've no other plans for tonight. So it would be great to have dinner with you and your father." The taut lines of his mouth eased as he smiled. "By all means, yes. I do want to spend this evening with you, Claudia." His smile now reached his eyes as he looked directly at her. "What time may I pick you up?" he asked, putting his empty pipe in his pocket. He rose from his chair and reached for her hands, then pulled her from her seat to stand close in front of him.

"Seven would be fine. I'll tell Dad that we'll meet him in the lounge at the Tulsa Club at seven-thirty."

He continued to hold both her hands warmly in his for another few seconds as his smile caressed her. "Your eyes are more blue than silver right at this minute, and I still haven't figured out what that says about the state of your emotions. Care to give me a clue?"

"Maybe I will later, but right now I'm not too sure myself."

"I'd be glad to help you find out." He pulled her to him, intending to take her in his arms.

Ducking her head, she edged back away from him. "I'm still on company time, Mr. Brad Hayes," she teased, laughing.

"Wait until I get you on your own time," he challenged her as he left.

Alone now in her office, she walked again to the window and stood, a perturbed expression creasing the corners of her eyes. There was no denying the animosity Brad felt toward her father. She wondered if she should have told Brad that she now knew Howard was the man responsible for Sam Hayes's leaving Tulsa. Maybe it would be a good idea to talk to him about it, but on the other hand, what possible good could it do? It was so long ago, and the problem was between Howard and Sam, not between her and Brad. Crossing her arms, she leaned her forehead against the cool window glass. It would help if she understood the whole affair, because she certainly prayed that, whatever the sins of their fathers had been, it wasn't going to spoil things between her and Brad. He was attracted to her; she knew that. She even believed he was beginning to care more than just a little for her. Surely she couldn't have such strong feelings about him if he didn't have them about her too. She might not be all that experienced, but she wasn't totally naive either.

Claudia turned, walked back to her desk and rested her hand on the telephone. Doubts needled her mind. Perhaps putting Brad and her father together at dinner tonight was not such a good idea. At least for the best results it should be a social evening and not business. But how could she manage that when Howard would be hoping to further the El-Sa deal for her?

A sudden shining thought illuminated her face. Uttering a pleased exclamation, she snatched up the phone. Why not suggest to her father that he invite Myra to have dinner with them too? After all, this was Myra's twentieth anniversary with the company. It would be a bona fide dinner party, a celebration that included two couples. She smiled broadly, warming enthusiastically to the great possibilities the evening might have in store for all four of them.

Claudia chose a melon-colored cocktail dress to wear that evening. "I had to prove to you that I don't always wear blue," she told Brad when he arrived at seven to pick her up.

He took his time inspecting her with admiring eyes, making note of how the scalloped edges of the bodice lay softly against her skin in a vee that was cut narrow but low, revealing a suggestion of the full rise of her breasts. The graceful contours of the skirt hugged her waist, then spread out in semifullness to swirl becomingly where it brushed against her slender, perfectly shaped legs.

"No matter what color it is, every man there tonight

will admire you in that dress," Brad commented, one sandy red eyebrow arched.

Claudia flinched at his words, wishing he'd said anything else, but not that she would attract the attention of other men. He'd meant it as a compliment; she knew that, of course. But still, his saying it the way he did brought the image of her mother to her mind. Vanessa, who desired that all men admire her. Claudia wanted one man's approving eyes on her tonight, only one, and she'd worn this dress because she was in a party mood. She had to admit that she'd also worn it because it was flattering and feminine and different from the tailored suits Brad had seen her in at the office. Lowering her head quickly, she hoped that what she was thinking was not revealed in her face.

Howard and Myra were already having a cocktail when Claudia and Brad joined them. Claudia made the introductions, and Howard immediately engaged Brad in a discussion of sailing, comparing the merits of Lake Keystone and similar-sized lakes in his state of Texas. While Brad handled his end of the conversation with seeming ease, Claudia could see the shimmering intensity in Brad's eyes as he noted everything about Howard Carlton with photographic detail.

It appeared as if both men were going to avoid the subject of oil production, and apparently neither of them intended mentioning the fact that Brad was the son of a man Howard had known and done business with in the past. When Claudia realized all of this, she relaxed and fell into animated woman talk with Myra.

Claudia had never seen Myra Allan look more attractive than she did that night. She was wearing a tawny beige silk dress, a shade perfect for her rich brown hair and magnolia-fair complexion. Maybe it was just Claudia's imagination, but she could swear that the radiant glow she'd seen on Myra that morning was even more pronounced now.

Leaving the lounge, the four of them went up one flight of stairs to the regal elegance of the Tulsa Club's ivory and gold dining room. A myriad of muted lights from the elaborate crystal and gilt chandeliers that hung from the high ceiling revealed numerous groups of diners. In a corner at the far end of the spacious room, a young man wearing a dinner jacket was playing the piano and crooning sentimental lyrics into a microphone suspended above the music rack.

Once they were seated at a table near the center of the room, Howard turned his attention to Myra. Claudia was pleased because now Brad was concentrating on her. She had a lot of things she hoped to talk to him about, knowing that tomorrow he'd be going back to Texas.

Their dinner orders were taken, and with the usual impeccable service, shrimp cocktails were served immediately followed by a delicious clear soup. Their entire meal was extraordinarily good, and the soft strains of the piano music in the background set a romantic mood which mingled with the hum of their conversation. Though Howard seemed to be enjoying himself as much as the rest of them, from time to time Claudia caught her father looking quizzically at Brad. Just as Brad had studied her father earlier, now Howard was observing Brad with thoughtful concentration. Her father was not a man who masked his feelings too well. Claudia could tell that something about Brad was bothering her father, bothering him a great deal indeed. She sensed instinctively that it stemmed from the fact that Brad was Sam Hayes's son.

The four of them lingered awhile over their dessert and coffee. Finally Claudia brought up the fact that tomorrow was, after all, a working day, and with that she and Brad excused themselves.

As they rose to leave, Claudia was taken aback when her father said, "I would welcome the sight of one of your father's rigs drilling on a Carlton Company lease again, Brad. So when you see Sam, I hope you'll tell him that for me."

After an entire evening without a mention of Sam Hayes, Claudia could scarcely believe that her father was doing so now. She shot a look at him, a warning light flickering in her eyes.

Brad appeared momentarily shaken by Howard's words, but he recovered with lightning speed. "I will tell him I met you, sir," he said with cool politeness, giving Howard a searching look, his brown eyes now as dark as strong boiled coffee—and as bitter. He paused, still regarding Howard; then, moving his head sharply, he spoke to Myra. "My father will be interested to hear that I helped you celebrate your twentieth year with your company." He smiled at her with his lips, but the smile never reached his eyes.

Claudia put her hand on Brad's arm, her fingers pressing tensely and wrinkling the worsted fabric of his suit coat. "We have to leave," she said, and tugged on his arm to urge him to follow her. Then she immediately turned and walked away from the table. She didn't look back over her shoulder to see if Brad was coming after her, but before she got to the large arched doorway, she felt his touch on her back. He let his hand rest between her shoulder blades until they entered the elevator, which would return them to the lobby of the Tulsa Club.

"I'd like to believe you broke away from Myra and your father because you were as anxious to be alone with me as I am to be alone with you." He had leaned close to her ear and whispered the words in a teasing manner. When she made no response, he straightened, his attitude immediately altering. "It was something more serious, wasn't it? You wanted to keep me from talking about Sam to your father and Myra, didn't you?"

She was able to avoid answering him because they had reached the lobby and three laughing, noisy couples were waiting for her and Brad to step off the elevator so they could take it.

Brad didn't refer to the subject again, and she was glad for that. She had the feeling that it would prove a mistake for them to discuss their fathers and the problems that had existed between them in the past. There was surely nothing that either of them would gain, nor would talking about it rectify the harm that had been done. Claudia didn't want this or anything to mar the relationship that could be developing between her and Brad, and the two drove home in a thoughtful silence.

"There was one thing wrong about this evening," Brad said as he followed Claudia through the front door of her apartment. "Do you know what it was?"

Claudia looked at him questioningly, feeling both mystified and wary. Was he going to ask her the same question he had in the elevator? "No, I don't think I do. And furthermore, I hate pro-and-con discussions about what was right and what was wrong following a party. Let's not rehash anything and spoil the pleasant time I had tonight."

Brad's tanned face was now lit with an easy smile. "If you'll get off that soapbox or whatever it is you're on, I'll explain that I was merely referring to that wonderful piano music we listened to during dinner. I simply think the evening would have been better if I could have had my arms around you and we'd danced."

"Oh," she said, chagrined.

He was still smiling. "Have you got a stereo?"

She nodded. "And a tape deck too. Over there." She pointed to a low cabinet with several shelves above it next to the television set. "Help yourself and I'll be right back." She disappeared down the hall, and when she returned five minutes later melodic strains of music sifted through the living room into the rest of the apartment.

"Dance with me," Brad said, holding his arms out to her as she reentered the room. Claudia walked into his arms and they began to sway together rhythmically to the music. After a few minutes Brad pulled her closer, holding her against him, and they moved together as the music flowed around them sensuously, languorously. Closing her eyes, Claudia gave herself up to the feeling of happiness that flooded through her. It felt wonderful to be held securely in Brad's arms as if she belonged there.

"I thought so," he said, his breath a warm caress where it touched the wing of her brow.

"Thought so what?" she murmured, opening her eyes.

"That we'd dance well together just like we do other things well together."

"Like sailing?"

He chuckled. "That too!" He kissed her temple and the edges of her soft hair where it fell across her forehead.

They had stopped dancing, but they still stood together. Brad kept one arm around her waist, lifting his other hand to touch her cheek. She did not move, but as she looked at him her blue eyes shimmered with silver light. He kissed her softly, his lips molding hers, brushing over them and returning. "I'm going to find it hard to be away from you for the rest of the week."

She felt a warm, melting sensation deep inside her caused by his kiss and the way he looked at her. "You'll be busy. You won't have time to think about me," she said, trying for the light touch that she knew she should try to keep with him.

"I'll think about you, all right, every time I see a brass candlestick or anything at all that's blue. And if it rains and the wind blows, then the image of my wind-tossed Oklahoma girl will be superimposed on everything I look at."

She opened her lips in a little whistling sigh. "You could sweep a girl off her feet with romantic talk like that."

"Could I?" He looked at her, his eyes faintly smiling. He kissed her deeply then, his hands sliding up under her hair to hold her head. There was no restraint in his kiss, and Claudia trembled in his arms, overwhelmed by the emotions sweeping through her. Her heart pounded against her ribs with heavy, labored beats. It was as if the world had fallen away and there was only the reality of this moment between them and the feel of his lips on hers. She kissed him back with an urgency that almost frightened her.

Her response caused his kiss to deepen with increasing passion. He was arousing desires and needs in her she couldn't control, didn't seem to want to control. It was there again—the electricity—the sparks that sent fire racing through her. A shudder that was both longing and apprehension quivered along every nerve in her body.

Brad released her slowly and, taking her cheeks in his hands, searched her face with questioning eyes. Neither of them spoke and Claudia had no idea how long they simply looked at each other. There was no longer any trace of a smile in Brad's eyes, only a questioning, seeking look and something else that Claudia didn't understand.

"I had better go," he said hoarsely. "I had better go

right now.'' He took his hands away from her face suddenly and took a step backward so they were no longer touching.

Bewildered, she pressed her cold fingers against her now trembling lips. What had happened? What was wrong? As soon as her mind formed the question, she sensed the answer. It was there in the deep lines she now noticed around Brad's mouth and in the tight, compressed set of his lips. She was what was wrong. More to the point, she was *who* was wrong. She was Claudia Carlton.

Chapter Five

Claudia pummeled her pillow one more time. Why couldn't she get in a position where she could relax and go to sleep? She would be exhausted at work in the morning. If only there were some way to force her mind to go blank. For the past hour or more, every time she closed her eyes she saw Brad's strong-boned face moving close to hers. It seemed that every nerve in her body had total recall of the secure pressure of his arms holding her and his mouth searching hers.

Turning her pillow over, she fluffed it up and then brushed her hand across it to smooth out the wrinkles. She could erase the creases in the pillowcase; what she couldn't erase were all the exquisite emotions Brad had stirred in her. They were locked away inside her heart where they would stay.

* * *

The next day Claudia asked Myra to meet her for lunch. As soon as they were seated at a table and had placed their order, Claudia leaned forward, an intent querying look on her face. "I want you to tell me everything you know about Sam Hayes. I have to understand what happened between him and my father."

Myra's eyes flared slightly. "That was such a long time ago, Claudia, and I hadn't been working for your father too long. I don't really know that there's too much I can tell you."

"Please, don't hedge with me. It's very important that I find out about this."

Myra avoided Claudia's gaze and toyed nervously with her silverware. "You should ask your father about it, you know, not me."

Claudia frowned. "I did. I asked him yesterday, but he only answered me with vague generalities. He said things like how important his family and this company are to him and that he found it necessary to go back on his verbal agreement with Brad's father. That really didn't explain anything." She pressed her hand to her brow and looked at her father's secretary with troubled eyes. "How could he have done something like that? To break a verbal contract is unfair, even dishonest. I can't believe my father had such a lack of integrity. Did Sam Hayes really deserve that?"

Myra hesitated, looking first at Claudia, then at the spoon she'd been scooting back and forth on the tablecloth in front of her. "I—I can't say."

Claudia felt as tense as a coiled spring. Why was Myra fencing with her about this? "Can't or won't?" she asked tersely, her frustration turning to anger. "Don't you understand? I have to know the details and the reason my father deliberately set out to ruin another man. Can't I make you see how important this is to me?''

"I think I'm just beginning to. It has something to do with you and Brad Hayes, doesn't it?''

Claudia nodded, blinking back the unbidden tears caused by her overwrought emotions. "I know it's crazy when I've only known him such a short time, but I feel something different for Brad, different and more exciting than anything I've felt for anyone before. I think I'm in love with him.''

"I'd say he cares something for you too,'' Myra said gently. "I saw signs of that last night.''

Claudia's hand crept to her throat. "I hope you're right, but I'm afraid that he's determined not to let himself care for the daughter of the man who set out to destroy his father. I wouldn't be surprised if Brad doesn't actually hate Dad. I know this: what happened to him and his parents eighteen years ago is still fresh and vivid in Brad's mind. It forms a barrier between us.''

"No it doesn't. That's the past, and it's best forgotten now. After all, Sam Hayes is a fighter like your father is. Sam's overcome the harm done to his business. He's successful again now. Doubly so, I'd say, with both a drilling company and an oil well supply company too. It seems both he and his son are doing well now,'' she said, smiling reassuringly. "And in defense of your father, I can tell you that he did what seemed the only thing he could do at the time. He discovered later that he'd been wrong, but at the time it was not entirely his fault. He believed what he was told and acted accordingly.'' Myra was looking at Claudia, but there was a faraway expression in the depths of her hazel eyes.

"What he was told? What does that mean?" Claudia asked, frowning curiously.

"Only that there was more involved than the wells that were being drilled. There were personal factors at stake."

Claudia kept her hand pressed to her throat, feeling the rapid beat of her pulse in the hollow underneath her fingers. "You're talking in riddles, Myra. I wish you'd stop."

"You're right, I am. I shouldn't have said as much as I did. What you should do is tell your father about your feelings for Brad Hayes. Then I think he'll be willing to tell you what happened and why. But I can't, and you mustn't ask me to. I'm an outsider, and this is a matter your father would want to explain to you himself." Myra's voice shook slightly and the distress she felt was revealed on her face. She grabbed up her napkin and spread it quickly over her lap, continuing to smooth the fold with her hands over and over.

Observing her, Claudia was struck with a sudden insight. From Myra's words and attitude it was apparent that she felt more for Howard Carlton than the mere respect and loyalty of a secretary for her boss. "I promise you I'll do just that," Claudia assured her with a quick smile as the waitress returned to serve them their lunch.

Myra gave a relieved sigh and picked up her fork. Claudia followed suit, but as she lifted the first bite, she paused with her fork halfway between her plate and her mouth. Her eyes had gone suddenly wide with a look of pleased speculation. She was remembering the other afternoon, when Myra had said that she had thought about getting married again but that the right man hadn't asked her. Was the right man Howard Carlton? Claudia had wondered at the time just who the right man might be. Now she strongly suspected that she knew exactly who he was. She put the forkful of mushroom crepe in her mouth and ate it. "Perfect, absolutely perfect," she said, her eyes sparkling like vivid blue sapphires.

Myra glanced over at her. "The crepe?"

Claudia gave a bright laugh. "That too!"

"So you met Howard Carlton?" Sam Hayes leaned forward in the dark maroon leather armchair, scowling heavily at Brad, who had just entered the library of his father's house and stood with one hand braced against the wide doorframe. "I bet that proved interesting to you."

"It proved interesting to both of us," Brad said, avoiding looking directly at his father by glancing around the mellow, mahogany-paneled walls of the darkly masculine room. "The fact is, I believe he was even more interested in knowing me than I was in him."

"How do you mean that?"

Brad shot his father a wry smile. "Carlton is curious as the devil about why you'd enter a business setup with his company again."

Sam's heavy brows arched over his sharp hazel eyes. "Was he, now? Did he say that?"

"No, he didn't discuss the lease deal at all, and that's the very reason I'm positive it bothers him. Oh, Carlton Petroleum is mighty anxious to have our mineral rights, all right, but Howard's worried that you and I might try to get retribution for what he did to you before."

Sam barked a scoffing laugh, then leaned back in his chair, his large hands clasped behind his head. "Well, I won't say I'm not enjoying knowing we have him worried a bit, but I've gotten over my need to get revenge on him. As a matter of fact, I may have even gotten over hating him as fiercely as I once did. Howard caused your mother and me a great deal of misery, but Carlton has had his share of pain and heartache too. That amoral wife of his put him through hell, and I can honestly say I feel sorry for him.''

"Well I don't!'' Brad declared hotly, angry color rising in his face. "And I want to make damn sure that El-Sa gets the best of this lease contract with his company.''

"And what do you consider the best?''

"Two thousand dollars an acre.''

"No need to be greedy, Brad. Anyway, two thousand is way out of the ball park. I'd say we'd be lucky to get twelve hundred. A thousand is actually a fair price. What did they offer?''

"They offered a thousand at first, and I said no deal.'' Brad crossed the room slowly, a smug smile on his face. "That was on Friday. By yesterday Claudia had talked Howard into letting her raise it to fifteen hundred.''

Surprise registered on Sam's rugged face. "That's a heck of a good figure. I'd never have believed that Howard would go that steep.''

"I think the reason is that this Stephens County operation has more potential than anything Claudia's handled before. She needs our lease badly. And, of course, she's his daughter and he's willing to stretch himself for her sake since she's handling the deal.''

"It sounds as if everything has worked to our advantage. They do agree to having Alamo rigs on all the wells?''

"Claudia went along with that from the start.'' Brad walked to one side of the massive oak desk at the back of the room. "This was on Friday, the first day we discussed the deal. Howard was out of town, and according to Claudia she was to handle this deal entirely on her own.'' He paused before continuing his explanation, placing his

hands on the large world globe that stood mounted on its
three-legged wooden stand to one side of Sam's antique
rolltop desk. He turned the globe slowly, lost in thought
for a moment. The globe was the thing he remembered
best from their big house in Tulsa. It had stood by the
bookcase in the living room of the home he'd loved, the
one where he'd grown up from birth to nearly his teens.
He kept his right hand resting lightly on top of it for a
while, even after it had ceased turning; then he walked
closer to his father's chair, picking up where he'd left off.
"By then I'd discovered that no one at Carlton knew what
El-Sa Corporation consisted of. Best of all, they didn't
know that El-Sa was Elizabeth and Sam Hayes." A grin
spread slowly across Brad's face. "Wouldn't you have
loved to see old Howard's reaction when he discovered
that bit of information?"

Sam's shaggy brows lifted over his hazel eyes in a look
of amusement. "Yeah," he said with a low chuckle. "I'd
have enjoyed being in on that. You can bet your life I
would."

Brad considered a large, overstuffed lounge chair with
an ottoman in front of it, the only comfortable seat in the
study. He eased himself into it, propping his feet up lazily
in front of him. He looked at ease with himself and with
his father for the first time since he'd entered his parents'
house when he arrived back in Abilene that evening.

"Dad, I guess now I have your okay to tell Claudia
Carlton we'll go ahead with the lease for fifteen hundred
dollars an acre, right?"

"You mean you didn't do that before you left Tulsa?"
Sam angled his head at his son, eyeing him curiously.
"Why on earth not?"

"I guess I wanted to stall on it. Also, it gives me an

excuse to take Claudia sailing again when I go back to Tulsa next weekend.'' Brad smiled and crossed his arms, wholly relaxed now.

Sam now held his chin between his thumb and forefinger, studying Brad's face intently. "This Claudia Carlton has made some impression on you, hasn't she?"

"As a matter of fact, she has."

Sam frowned. "How much of an impression?"

"More than Howard Carlton cared to see, that's for sure. Last night at dinner he looked at me with that 'you're the last man in the world I'd want my daughter to get mixed up with' look."

"And is she someone you're mixed up with?"

"Claudia is a special kind of girl."

"That's not what I asked." Sam's gruff voice was subdued, quiet.

Brad's eyes were unwavering, his expression inscrutable. "It's what I wanted you to know, Dad. Claudia is beautiful, exciting and special. You'd like her."

Sam straightened in his chair. "Not with the Carlton name, I wouldn't." His mouth thinned in a bitter line. "I want you to stick to business with her, Brad. This is a good deal for us and we'll come out on top with it. So let's take Howard's money and just leave his daughter alone." He stood up suddenly and walked over to stand directly in front of Brad's chair. "I'm telling you a fact, so listen to me. Hayes and Carlton—it's like water and oil. They never will mix, so don't try it. All you'll do is pollute the water."

A delivery truck was stopped in front of Claudia's apartment, and as she drove up the driver jumped out and hurried over to her. "Are you Miss Claudia Carlton?" he asked her. Claudia nodded. "Oh, good." The boy sounded relieved. "I've got flowers for you that were ordered to be delivered after five o'clock."

Waxy green florist's paper ballooned around the vase of flowers the delivery boy handed to her. Claudia carried them quickly inside her apartment and set the vase down on the dining room table, then excitedly stripped away the protective covering. At the sight of the cobalt blue vase filled with yellow roses and blue delphinium, she uttered an exclamation of delight. Her fingers shook as she removed the card attached to the roses, slipping the card from the small white envelope. "They don't grow blue roses, but I got everything else in blue. Brad." Reading Brad's words caused happiness to bubble up inside her and spill through her parted lips in a whispered sigh.

He'd been thinking about her before he headed back to Texas, there was no doubt of that. She leaned over and inhaled the delicate scent of the roses, feeling enormously pleased. Picking up the deep blue glass vase, she carried it to the living room and placed the flowers in the center of the coffee table. As she did so, she hesitated for a second, wondering if perhaps Brad had sent the roses as a sort of thank-you because her father had taken them to dinner last night. Was it merely one of those good-business-relations gestures? Claudia pressed her lips together so hard they hurt; she was annoyed that she was allowing such a thought to diminish her joy. Why did she let herself reduce Brad's thoughtful act to a business tactic? Was it because she was anticipating what her father's attitude was going to be? He would probably tell her that Brad's only concern was what was advantageous to Alamo Drilling and Sam Hayes, and that Brad's attentions to her were manipulative means to gain his own ends.

Claudia turned away from the coffee table and marched to the kitchen to put something in the microwave for her dinner. Maybe it was just as well that Howard had been out of town today so she couldn't talk to him about Brad. She wasn't willing to have her father prejudice her thinking or destroy the sentimental, romantic way she felt. She wanted to believe that Brad had been thinking about her before he left Tulsa and that he had stopped at the florist, selecting not only the flowers but the cobalt blue vase.

A smile moved on her lips again, and she pressed her fingers to her mouth as if to hold the smile and keep the happy feeling that accompanied it from vanishing again in a parade of negative thoughts.

It was the middle of the afternoon the following day before Claudia heard from her father. "I found a note on my desk saying you wanted to see me," her dad said on the phone. "Come up whenever you like. I'll be here in my office the rest of the afternoon."

He sounded in a particularly good mood, Claudia thought. With luck this would turn out to be the perfect time to catch him relaxed and talkative.

"I want to thank you for being so great the other night at dinner," she said as she sailed into his office, smiling.

"It turned out to be a nice evening all the way around, and I was interested in meeting Brad Hayes. He's very much like his father, I think."

"Brad *is* an interesting man, and I enjoyed all the time I spent with him. We discovered we like many of the same things," Claudia said, her eyes curving upward as she smiled, recalling the sailing and then dinner at the all-green restaurant.

"Well, if you've made your deal with him, it was time well spent."

"It wasn't all business, Dad. I find I like Brad a lot."

Howard gave her a gauging look. "In his case, I would definitely prefer that you didn't mix pleasure with business."

"Why do you say that?"

"I have some reservations about him, that's why." The planes of his face hardened and there was now a defensive thrust to the angle of his jaw. "It has to do with the gut feeling I've had for years that Sam Hayes would someday seek retribution from me."

"So—does that need to involve Brad? I don't feel that it does." Claudia stood stiffly facing her father, her hands clasped tightly in front of her. "I really like Brad." She hesitated, lowering her lashes so her eyes wouldn't reveal the true depth of her feelings to her father. "And I believe that Brad isn't altogether unaware of me, either. I don't want what took place years ago to stand between Brad and me now."

She heard her father's sharp intake of breath, but he didn't say a word to her. Instead, he walked a few steps away, then turned around and came back to where she stood. Putting both of his hands on her shoulders, he said. "I don't ever want to see you get hurt, honey, or even disappointed. So be careful. Take plenty of time to truly know this man before you decide whether he's important to you." He squeezed her in a gentle hug and let her go. She knew that he didn't intend to say or do anything further. If he might have told her what had happened to cause the rift between him and Brad's father, he wasn't going to now.

Claudia returned to her office and put her mind on her

work. For the rest of that week, the subject of Sam Hayes was avoided.

Claudia opened the door and Brad was there. She was filled with an incomparable sense of joy. If she'd had doubts about the depth of her feelings for him before, she could have none now. Just the sight of his tall, lanky frame filling her doorway made her breathless as if she'd been running fast and hard for quite a distance.

When he continued to stand there, smiling at her, she extended her hands to pull him inside. He took her hands, pulling her to him. "I didn't drive all the way from Texas to stand here holding your hands," he said just before kissing her determinedly on the mouth.

Claudia's arms came up around his neck, and she kissed him back with reckless abandon, aware only of a potent sense of exhilaration, a joy that needed to be expressed.

When he let her go, he smiled, looking at her as if he wanted to absorb the sight of her completely. "That was a nice welcome. Almost worth going away in order to come back for." He traced the soft fullness of her lips with his thumb. "I told someone this week that you were special. You are, you know." He kissed the corners of her mouth, then brushed his lips teasingly over hers again.

She closed her eyes as he kissed her, then opened them slowly and smiled up at him. "If I'm so special, why are you standing there with the door open as if you weren't sure you wanted to stay?"

"Because we're not staying. In fact, you and I are leaving right now so that we'll have time to eat our share of barbecue before the performance starts."

Claudia's eyes widened in astonishment. "Is what you just said supposed to make sense to me?"

Brad grinned. "Not really. It's a surprise. I ordered tickets for this season's opening performance at Discoveryland before I left Tulsa. They were already sold out, but they promised to save me any cancellations. I didn't know until I got back in town that they'd been able to get seats for us for tonight."

"Opening night!" she exclaimed, her rising inflection mirroring her pleased excitement. "That's special."

"No, you're special. I already told you that." He gently pushed her away from him. "Now go gather up whatever feminine paraphernalia you have to have, so we can get there before all the ribs and baked beans are gone." He shoved her down the hall toward her bedroom. "You've got five minutes, no more."

They drove to Discoveryland, the outdoor amphitheater located in the rolling hills of northeastern Oklahoma a short distance from Tulsa, and were met by Western-clad parking attendants on horseback who directed them to the already well-filled parking area.

It was the first week in June, and the Oklahoma summer was beginning. The day had been a warm one, with a high temperature of eighty-seven degrees. Now, however, as the sun began to lower, Claudia could feel a light, cooling breeze stirring. The pungent odor of hickory-smoked barbecue permeated the air as they walked to the cleared area in the center of a glade where the food was being served. As soon as they had each filled a plate with barbecued ribs, baked beans and cole slaw, then piled a couple of thick slices of the savory, lightly grilled Western-style toast atop the ribs, they found two empty places at one of the long, wood plank picnic tables.

An hour or so later the purple shadows of the descending evening caused everyone to vacate the picnic tables and head out along the paths that led to the large outdoor theater, for it was time for the preliminary entertainment to begin. At the center of the stage was a group of performers in Western dress, the young men in jeans and cowboy hats and boots, vivid red bandannas knotted around their necks, and the pretty girls in rainbow-colored calico dresses, their long hair tied with matching pastel hair bows. They were performing hill country clog dances and singing catchy, rhythmic songs.

A bit later, when the last rays of twilight had faded into the Oklahoma summer night, the production of the American classic *Oklahoma* came alive on Discoveryland's natural hillside stage. Cowboys raced in on horseback, and a covered wagon thundered across a wooden plank bridge as the sounds of the spirited Rodgers and Hammerstein music filled the June night.

Once the show was under way, Brad spread his arm across the back of Claudia's chair. And when the leading players were singing 'People Will Say We're in Love,' he pressed his hand around her shoulder affectionately.

Claudia tried to force her attention back to the play, but a heady feeling was causing her mind to spin. Maybe he was beginning to suspect that she might be falling in love with him. She didn't want that—not yet—not before he had given her some reason to hope that he could really care for her too. But was that going to happen? Or did Brad think of her only as someone he could have a casual relationship with when he happened to be in Tulsa? A temporary affair like that was something Vanessa would have accepted, even sought. Claudia cringed, a shudder trembling her shoulders.

Brad pressed her shoulder warmly. "Are you getting cold?" he asked, concerned.

She didn't look at him, but merely shook her head mutely, avoiding conversation with him until she could put a tight rein on her thoughts and emotions.

Chapter Six

The rousing finale of *Oklahoma* seemed to keep echoing through the hillside as Claudia and Brad trudged the long, winding path back to the parking area. It was a mild evening, and the moon was only a pale silver crescent against the black night sky. Brad held her hand, and they ambled back slowly as if they were reluctant to leave the restful wooded surroundings and return to the noisy city.

Although it was late when they got back to Claudia's apartment, she offered to make coffee for them and even thaw and heat a pecan coffee cake.

"Don't you want to save your coffee cake for breakfast?" Brad asked, following her into the kitchen.

"I have more than one," she assured him. "I keep at least two in the freezer most of the time. They're my secret sin." She opened the freezer compartment of her refrigerator as she said this, and pulled out a round foil pan.

Brad scrutinized her with amusement. "You're lucky the wages of your sin don't show, at least anyplace that I can see." He grabbed hold of her, shaping her midriff with his hands.

Before he could move his hands over her even more intimately, Claudia twisted away from him and, opening the oven, thrust the cake inside and set the timer. "We'll have to wait awhile for that to heat through and for the coffee to perk."

"Good." Brad took her hand and led her out of the kitchen and over to the couch in the living room. "I've got some plans to make with you. I've been counting all week long on getting back here to Tulsa to spend the whole weekend with you."

"I was counting on that too." She didn't attempt to be at all coy with him. She sat down on the sofa and stretched her legs out comfortably in front of her, kicking off her pumps and crossing her ankles. "A thoughtful man who's discerning enough to send me pretty roses in a blue vase is my choice for a weekend companion every time."

Brad's strong-boned face seemed to crack into warm creases and his bright eyes held hers with an intent look. "We're in perfect agreement then." He put his arm around her, fitting her warmly against the hollow of his shoulder. "I planned for us to be at Keystone tomorrow, go swimming and sailing, maybe take a picnic lunch over to one of the shady coves."

"That sounds nice, but I do have an alternate suggestion." She fingered the button on the cuff of Brad's oxford cloth shirt.

"What's that?"

"We could go up to our place on Grand Lake O' the Cherokees. We've got a sailboat at our dock—two, in fact. We're located on a point with a deep cove to each side, perfect picnic spots and great swimming. And there's lots of activity at the yacht club on Saturday night with a band for dancing.'' She talked fast, running her words together.

Brad had been kissing her hair at the edge of her forehead, and now he feathered kisses on the arch of her cheek. ''Sounds like there are a lot of fun things to do up there. I imagine we could stay busy all day Saturday and Sunday.'' He bent his head and teased her by nuzzling the tender area just below her ear.

''We could stay the whole weekend and come back Monday morning early if you like,'' she said, a tentative note in her voice, as if she were uncertain whether to say that or not.

Brad moved his shoulder, turning her around in his arms so he could look directly into her face. ''I'd like that more than anything.''

Brad's handsome face was just a breath away from hers and his eyes were filled with an unmistakable look of desire. Claudia lowered her lashes, wanting to hide her own answering emotion. ''The lake house is large, three bedrooms and two baths. We can share it and keep out of each other's way, I think,'' she said with a mildly self-conscious laugh.

''I'm certain that it's far larger than either of us needs.''

Claudia looked up at him through the protective screen of her thick lashes. Brad was studying her face with eyes that had gone darkly passionate. Slowly he put his mouth on hers. An intoxicating warmth swept over her as his lips met hers with an urgent insistence. Her lips parted beneath his, and as their kiss deepened, so did the pressure of his body against hers. She circled her arms around him, trailing her fingers sensually along the back of his neck. This made Brad shift his hand lower on her back to bring her even more urgently against him. She felt him ease her down so she was lying against the soft cushions of the sofa. Then he lightly drew his fingers across her breast, stroking her with a softness that was like the brush of a butterfly's wings and more powerfully exciting than any imperative touch could ever have been. She opened her eyes to see the look of ardent appraisal he was giving her. She felt the overpowering joy of loving him.

His hand lingered on her breast, and she lifted her hand to touch his face. She smoothed her fingers over his high, strong cheekbone. The little nerve below Brad's eye jerked as her finger accidently pressed it. When she slid her hand across his chin and let it lay curved around the side of his neck, he lowered his head and kissed her forehead, then drew a line of kisses along her brow and down her cheek.

Within her, desire flowed with a warm insistence, and a soft, murmuring sound came from deep in her throat.

"I can feel your heart," Brad whispered, his voice husky with emotion. His hand now covered her breast, and the look in his brown eyes stopped the breath in her throat. "Claudia, I want to make love with you." Brad's voice was deep, heavy with desire. "I want to hold you, touch you, feel you all over." His mouth slid passionately down the warm soft skin of her throat, and she could feel his body trembling against her own and feel his heart hammering against the strong wall of his chest.

He lifted his face from the hollow of her neck so he could kiss her lips once more. For a moment it was a gentle caress of his mouth on hers, but only for a moment, and then it changed until it was more than just a kiss. It was a searching and a hungry wandering of his hands sliding over her, seeking, touching. . . .

A desperate yearning overcame Claudia as a deep

longing that had lain dormant before now swept over her. She trembled in Brad's arms, responding to him, kissing him, touching him now with a need of her own. She was oblivious to everything but the two of them, the exciting warmth of their bodies clinging together.

Suddenly the sharp, insistent buzzing of the oven timer stabbed her into awareness. Abruptly she pulled her mouth from his and sat up.

"What the heck is that?" Brad demanded, his broad shoulders tense, his breathing ragged.

"The timer on the oven," she said, taking a deep breath to slow her racing heartbeat. "And I'm afraid it will keep on buzzing until you let me up so I can go to the kitchen and turn it off." Her hands momentarily touched his arm in concern, and there was apology in her voice when she said, "I'm sorry, Brad, but that's the signal that the coffee cake is ready for us to eat."

Brad looked at her steadily, his mouth set in a humorless smile. "And just think, they called Romeo and Juliet the star-crossed lovers. And we haven't got it as good as they did, because we have both intangible and tangible things conspiring to keep us apart," he said caustically as he moved to allow Claudia to leave the sofa.

Claudia looked puzzled. A ringing timer was something tangible, and certainly disruptive, but she wondered exactly what he meant by the intangible things. What were they? Was he being facetious talking about Romeo and Juliet? What was he really implying with his cryptic statement? She had the sudden intuitive feeling that she would be happier not knowing, so without saying anything more she hurried into the kitchen.

They ate the cinnamon and pecan cake seated at the table in Claudia's dining room. Brad made plans with her for their drive to Grand Lake the next day as he ate and quickly drank a mug of coffee. When the mantel clock bonged twelve times, Brad drained the last of his coffee and stood up. "I think that clock of yours is issuing another of your warning signals," he said with a shrug. "Anyhow, it's time I was heading over to Lake Keystone and my lakeside hideaway." He had regained his usual easy manner with her, an he put his arm affectionately around her shoulders as they walked together to the door. He hesitated for a second, acting as if he might be going to kiss her good night, but he evidently changed his mind. Instead, he let his hands slide down her arms slowly, then took both of her hands in his, pressing them tightly. Then he was gone.

Claudia stood there in the hall after he left, staring absently at the closed door. There were a number of things she didn't understand about Brad, and that gave her misgivings about spending the weekend with him at the lake house. There was so much more she needed to know about him. They had talked about the surface things and she had had intriguing glimpses of a man for whom she had not been prepared. Was that why her father had cautioned her about Brad? Her father had intimated that Brad would disappoint her, even that he was capable of hurting her. Howard was someone who knew firsthand how deeply a person can be hurt by someone they love. This made him overly concerned, overly protective. With a frown pinching the bridge of her nose, she turned and went back to the kitchen to put the remaining coffee cake away and unplug the electric coffee pot.

Claudia turned out all the lights but the one on the table beside the sofa and went to her room to get ready for bed. She wasn't sleepy; indeed, she doubted if she'd be able to go to sleep at all. Still keyed up over all that had happened, she wasn't sure what to make of any of it. The entire evening had been too much. She'd been an emotional fool, blown up like a balloon and swept away by momentary passion.

Deciding to start behaving sensibly, she placed her overnight case on top of the bed and began to pack her bathing suit, shorts and knit shirts she'd need for sailing. She'd mentioned to Brad that they could go dancing Saturday night at the yacht club or they could go over to the Lakeside Supper Club if he preferred. Thinking of that, she packed a pair of slender strapped sandals and a turquoise pima cotton sundress.

When she had everything packed that she could possibly wear in one weekend, she could find no further excuse to delay her going to bed. Convinced that she would be tossing and turning all through the night, she laid her head reluctantly on her pillow. Five minutes later she was sound asleep.

The persistent ringing of the telephone on the nightstand beside her bed jarred her awake. Lifting the receiver, she mumbled an indistinct, "Hello."

"Good morning, lazy lady. I woke you up, didn't I?"

"Uhh-umm, what makes you think that?" She fluttered her eyes open slowly and at the same time struggled to sit up in bed.

"That sexy, sleepy tone of your voice, that's what. Besides the fact that the phone had to ring nine times before you awoke enough to answer it."

"I'm sorry, Brad. I guess I forgot to set my alarm. What time is it anyway?"

"Eight-thirty, and I'm going to be after you at nine

o'clock sharp. We want to be out on that lake sailing before noon, you know.''

Claudia yawned audibly. ''Whoa, you'll have to hold on awhile. Don't pick me up until at least ten. I've got to go to the supermarket and pick up some food to take up to the house before I'll be ready to leave Tulsa.''

''No way. You forget that and just get yourself ready to leave. I'm taking care of the food shopping. I'll have everything for a picnic lunch plus all the food we're going to eat all weekend. Not only have I already planned the meals, but I plan to surprise you by cooking for you. How does that strike you?''

''Are you telling me you're a chef as well as a sailor?'' Her incredulity showed in her voice.

''I am,'' he boasted.

''What other talents do you have that I don't suspect?''

''None that I care to list over the telephone,'' he answered, teasing her with a rich, sensuous laugh. ''And none that you don't suspect.'' He laughed again, and hung up quickly before she had a chance to offer any comeback.

Claudia was laughing now too. She swung her legs over the edge of the bed, jumped up and hurried into the bathroom to take her shower. She liked waking up to Brad's jokes and banter, and certainly she was enjoying the fact that he'd made plans for all their meals for the weekend. It intrigued her, too, learning not only that he knew how to cook, but that he was going to do so for her. Stepping under the warm spray of water, she began to hum one of the melodic songs from last night's performance of *Oklahoma*, ''Oh What a Beautiful Morning.'' She thought it was good that she was learning new things about Brad, that they were making discoveries about each other. She wanted to believe that they were building a bridge of small intimacies that could span the river of intangible things that continued to separate them.

It had been a long while since Claudia had made a trip up to the lake house, and now, with Brad doing the driving, she sat relaxed in the front seat beside him, gazing out the window at the green countryside. This area was the heart of Oklahoma's "green country," and the low rolling hills were dotted with blackjack oak and native pecan trees and the smaller picturesque redbuds and dogwoods.

Traffic was moderately heavy, but they made excellent time. Claudia knew without looking at the speedometer that Brad was driving well over the speed limit, for less than an hour and a half after they left Tulsa they were following the natural wild beauty of the shoreline, turning into the winding road that wound along the rocky cliffside to reach the house.

"No one's been up here in the past few months, so we'll have to open up and air it all out, maybe even have to knock down a few cobwebs," Claudia said as Brad parked the car where the road ended at a large cleared area at the back of the house. "I'll do that and make up the beds while you unload the car. And create a superb picnic lunch for us to take sailing as you promised," she added, giving him an impish grin.

Brad leaned across her to release the door on her side for her. When he straightened, he paused long enough to brush the side of her cheek with his knuckles. "Don't think I won't," he answered.

"I'm counting on it. After all, you didn't allow me time this morning to eat breakfast. I'm warning you, after a swim and even a brief sail, I'll be famished." She jumped out of the car, heading for the house.

Situated high above the lake amid mature trees, the house had a massive redwood deck that wrapped around the front and both sides. Claudia entered at the back, moving quickly through the kitchen to the main living area in the front. She opened the set of sliding glass doors, which led out to the deck, and then quickly walked around raising all the woven wood shades, which had been hung at the windows to prevent the sun's rays from fading the furniture when the house was not in use. She unlatched and lifted the windows, and a breeze like a mild tornado swept through the house, carrying away the musty odor of stale air and the acrid smell of the charred ashes that still remained in the huge natural stone fireplace.

She could hear Brad noisily opening cupboards in the kitchen as he put away the supplies he'd brought. She took sheets from a linen closet in the hall off the living room and went in to make up the double bed in the main bedroom located on the lower floor of the house.

Brad appeared in the doorway to the bedroom with her suitcase in his hand. "Where do you want this?"

Claudia had a pillow tucked under her chin and was putting a blue flowered case on it. "There by the door is fine." She placed the pillow at the head of the bed and began to fit the matching case on the second pillow.

"Where would you like me to bunk?"

"Take your pick of either of the bedrooms upstairs in the loft. The one toward the back of the house is the larger, but the front one has a view of the lake."

"That sounds nice. I'll take the front then." He walked closer to the bed and stood watching her as she smoothed the blue and green spread on top of the bed, tucking it neatly under the pillows. "You're pretty expert at that. I think I'd enjoy lying in a bed you'd made, even one with blue flowered sheets." He came closer, making a playful lunge toward her as if he were going to push her down on the bed she'd just finished making.

Sidestepping him artfully, she brushed past him, heading for the door. "I'll do equally as expert a job on your bed upstairs, and I'll use blue and white stripes, masculine and nautical. That should suit you better." She disappeared through the door and headed upstairs.

"We'll have an in-depth discussion about what will suit both of us while we're out sailing," he shouted after her, laughing.

A half hour later, Claudia joined Brad at the cove below the house where the sailboats were docked. Stowing away her beach bag and the towels she'd carried to the boat, she offered assistance in stepping the mast. While they worked together rigging the sails, Claudia described the area of the lake where she thought they should take a swim before they ate lunch.

The sun, which in the earlier morning hours had spread a soft golden glow over the water, had changed to a brilliant blaze reflecting brightly off the surface of the blue lake.

"The air is hot, but this water is cold beneath the surface," Brad warned when they reached the spot Claudia had chosen. "Are you sure you're game for a swim?"

"I am if you are," she challenged, tossing the anchor over the side to further emphasize her determination.

Brad dropped the sail. The next minute, he stripped off his jeans, disclosing maroon bathing trunks. His broad-shouldered body was slightly tanned, and a light mat of rusty red hair curled across his chest.

"You've already got a good start on a suntan; I thought redheads always burned." Claudia followed his lead, taking off her navy shorts and untying the tails of the white shirt she had knotted underneath her breasts.

"Not if they have brown eyes, they don't. I'm lucky; I'm not fair skinned like blue-eyed redheads." He gazed at her in open admiration as she removed the shirt, revealing that she was wearing an electric blue one-piece bathing suit that set off her slim, mature body to perfection. "How about you? I hope you won't burn any of that lovely exposed area." He tilted his head to one side and lifted that eyebrow.

"Don't worry. I won't. I use a suntan lotion, and besides, I intend to put my clothes back on over my suit as soon as I get out of the water."

"Worse luck," he growled, shaking his head at her. "And here I was counting on ogling you in that blue bathing suit all the rest of the afternoon." He slid neatly over the side of the boat into the water, then steadied it while she slipped into the water beside him. The water was cold, colder than she had anticipated even with Brad's warning. They stayed close to the boat, swimming away a few yards and then turning and heading back. Brad was a more energetic swimmer than she was. While he made a wide sweeping circle around the boat, she stayed off the bow and floated lazily on her back, moving her arms and legs just enough to keep her afloat. In a few minutes he was back, and he flipped over on his back and floated alongside her.

"You make a beautiful water sprite, but I'll have to be the first to admit that this water is too blasted cold for just lazing around in. What do you say we quit and go find a nice place to eat our lunch?"

Claudia immediately turned over, dog-paddling to get close enough to grab hold of the side of the boat. "I was turning blue all over," she said, scrambling aboard. She grabbed for a towel and tossed it to Brad, then began to rub herself vigorously with another.

Brad hung his towel around his neck while he hoisted the mainsail. Claudia had already lifted anchor, so while Brad handled the boat, she tucked her legs under her and, bending her head down, ran her fingers through her hair, separating the strands so the sun-warmed air would dry it.

They sailed close to shore, passing by a number of anglers fishing for bass where there was a thick base of willow trees growing at the edge of the water. When they discovered a shady cove surrounded with willows, but without the fishermen, they secured their boat and Brad produced a cooler of beer and soft drinks and a dark green plastic storage bag.

"That looks suspiciously like a trash bag. This is no time to play some kind of joke on me." She crossed her arms across her stomach to indicate that she was suffering pangs of starvation. "I pray you're going to tell me that bag is filled with delicious goodies that you labored to prepare for our sumptuous picnic." She made a woebegone face. "I shall die of hunger here and now if it isn't."

Brad laughed at her histrionics. "I'm not going to tell you that it's all of those things, but it is our lunch. I hope you're not going to be disappointed." He pulled two slender white sacks from the bag and handed one to her.

Claudia looked puzzled for an instant as she opened the paper bag to discover the contents. Her surprised gaze whipped to Brad's face. "It's a submarine sandwich." Her face crinkled with suppressed laughter. "Brad Hayes, you're a fraud. You didn't make our lunch, you bought it. While I was airing out the house and making the beds, I thought you were slaving in the kitchen creating lunch. What a sham you are.''

"I resent being called undeserved names," he said, pretending she had hurt his feelings. Giving her a sad, hangdog look, he went on, "If you'll remember, I only promised to provide your meals this weekend. I did not specify that I would create them *in toto*." He extended his hand to her. "Give it back. You don't have to eat it." He took hold of her wrist as if he might be going to take the sandwich from her.

"No, no, no. I like it. I want it." She jerked her hand away from him and, thrusting one end of the long bun into her mouth, bit off a good-sized hunk of the meat-filled sandwich. "A submarine is my favorite and it's de-lish-uuus." She talked with her mouth full and garbled her words as she chewed.

Brad examined her face, laughter lighting his eyes. Answering laughter danced in Claudia's eyes. The mood was set between them, and it carried through for the rest of the day. There was complete ease between them, and it was if they had a tacit understanding that they were spending this time together as romantic friends, nothing more. Brad exerted some sort of indefinable hold on her attention, and yet he made no move to touch her other than in a casual way. The sexual magnetism was there, but there had to be more to their relationship than that for Claudia. She now sensed that there had to be more for Brad as well, and this kindled sparks of hope within her heart. Was it possible that neither she nor Brad was willing to rush into intimacy until each was certain that they felt needs and desires that only the other could fulfill?

It was late in the afternoon before they brought the sailboat back into the dock below the house. As they climbed the hill to the house, Claudia warned Brad that she intended to take a long shower and shampoo and dry her hair before she got dressed for dinner.

"Take all the time you need," he said, pressing his hand into the small of her back to help her up the incline. "I'll keep busy fixing your dinner. After the razzing you gave me because I bought those submarine sandwiches, I have to prove to you that I can create dinner all on my own." He gave her a slight shove to emphasize his words.

"You mean we're not having a box of the colonel's fried chicken?" She tossed the words over her shoulder as she scurried ahead of him to reach the steps leading to the front deck of the house.

Brad ran after her and gave her a light swat on her backside. "No! We are not having some commercial fried chicken, Miss Smarty Pants."

She ran up the remaining steps, laughing. "Then I bet you bought us a frozen pizza. And I guess that will be okay, because next to foot-long sandwiches, I do go for Italian food."

"You're really asking for it, Claudia." There was a warning note in Brad's voice. Suddenly he grabbed hold of her waist, spinning her around to encase her firmly in his arms. "You've carried your razzing too far." He kissed her then, full on the mouth, silencing her by the driving force of his mouth. The playful, teasing scene between them now took on an entirely new dimension as Brad crushed her lips with compelling demand and with undeniable passion. His warm lips parted hers, and his hands slid lower, pressing her hard against him so that she was held immobile in his strong embrace.

Brad had never kissed her with quite this intensity before, and a surge of hot blood rushed to her head and spread like fire rapidly through her body. As his mouth searched hers, she responded involuntarily at first, then with complete consciousness. She grew aware that she had been waiting, even hoping for this moment when her body was molded so intimately to Brad's and his mouth was hungrily seeking hers.

Chapter Seven

They stood locked together for an endless moment, the desire they both felt threatening to overcome them completely.

Finally he released her, moving his face back just far enough to be able to look into her eyes. His breathing was shallow, his deep brown eyes shadowed and intent. "Now, I don't want to hear you mention food of any kind until you're seated at the table ready to eat the dinner I'm going to prepare for you. Is that understood?" His voice was husky.

She nodded mutely, the state of her emotions making her incapable of speech. Her pulse was still racing from the intensity of her feelings for Brad. Maybe it was just as well that she couldn't speak, for she had a wild urge at that minute to tell Brad how she felt about him. To say, "Brad, I love you. I love you and I want you and I've never felt or said this before to any man." But Brad's arms were no longer around her, his hands were no longer caressing her, for he had turned away and started off in the direction of the kitchen.

Gazing after him, she pulled her bottom lip between her teeth, perturbed by her thoughts. For no apparent reason she was recalling how her father had cautioned her about Brad, telling her that she must truly know him before deciding he was important to her. Her father had planted seeds of doubt in her mind by intimating that Brad could disappoint her, even hurt her deeply. Could he? More to the point, would he? Claudia frowned, disturbed that she would think of this now.

Turning away abruptly, she marched into her bedroom, stripped off her shorts and bathing suit and headed for the shower. She was still concerned about her father's attitude toward her relationship with Brad as she poured shampoo on her hair and whipped it into a thick lather. She began to massage her head fiercely as if she could scrub the worrisome, negative thoughts from her mind.

Once out of the shower, Claudia took a brush and the blow-dryer to her hair, adeptly styling it in a loose cap of soft curls. Looking at herself in the mirror, she grimaced wryly. It was plain to see that she'd gotten more sun than she'd bargained for, being out on the lake for so many hours today. She took pains applying a light foundation on her face, hoping it would place a matte finish over the pink shine the sun had placed on her nose and forehead. Pleased with the results, she smiled and went to work accenting her eyes with liner and a touch of eye shadow in the same shade of turquoise as the sundress she'd brought to wear that night.

When she had finished dressing, she walked over to look out the bedroom window that faced the redwood deck. She hadn't realized how long she'd taken to bathe and dress. The sky was streaked now with the gentle mauve shadows of the fading summer dusk. She turned back to check her appearance once more in the mirror over the dresser. She took one more minute to apply the jasmine fragrance she always wore to her throat and wrists. For good measure, she sprayed the scent in a halo around her hair and then strode out of her room and across the living room in search of Brad.

As she passed the open sliding glass doors, she caught the odor of burning hickory chips and charcoal from the cooker at the far end of the deck. She smiled. She might not know Brad's dinner menu, but apparently something was going to be charcoal broiled.

"Brad, are you out on the deck?" she shouted through the open door.

"No, I'm in the kitchen, but I'll be right in."

The living room appeared murky in the purple twilight. Claudia wandered around turning on a couple of table lamps and the swag light that hung over the game table in the corner of the room opposite the fireplace. Brad entered the living room carrying a small black laquered tray, which held two stemmed cocktail glasses.

"Good evening, madam," he greeted her with a formal nod in the manner of a maitre d'. "If it's agreeable, I'd be pleased to serve cocktails now."

"Thank you, Bradley. I'd like that, but on one condition. I never drink alone, so will you join me?" She played his game, offering a Mona Lisa smile.

"Whatever my lady wishes."

His rakish smile made her laugh as she took the glass he offered.

"Do you like a vodka martini, very dry?"

Claudia put the glass to her lips and tasted it. "I like this one." Cupping her hand more securely, she took another sip to lower the level of the liquid before walking over to sit down on one of the love seats that flanked the stone fireplace. She didn't want to tell Brad that she never drank martinis because they had been her mother's favorite drink. Her mind now conjured up the picture of Vanessa at some party at the country club, looking provocatively over the rim of her martini glass at some new man and laughing at him in that intimate, inviting way of hers. Claudia looked at the drink in her hand and then at Brad, who stood leaning his shoulder against the corner of the fireplace. When he saw her look over at him, he raised his glass.

"To my special girl, who's especially pretty tonight in another blue dress."

She tensed imperceptibly. "Am I really your special girl?" she asked.

"Didn't I say you were?"

"You said yesterday that you'd told someone else I was special. Who was it?"

He appeared taken aback by her direct question. Either that, or he didn't recall telling her. He took another drink of his martini before he finally answered her. "I was talking to my father about you. I told him you were special, that he would like you."

Her fingers convulsed tightly around the glass in her hand. "He wouldn't really like me, though, would he? He couldn't bring himself to like the daughter of Howard Carlton no matter how special you thought she was."

Brad's expression altered, hardened. "You know now, don't you? You know it was your father who drove us out of Tulsa." He looked at her, his eyes tiger bright.

She nodded, one hand moving up to circle her throat.

She stared at Brad's implacable expression. He hates my father, she thought. The hatred he felt as a boy is still buried deep inside him. She heaved a pained sigh. "Dad did a rotten thing to your father, and neither you nor I understand why. I'm sorry, Brad. I honestly believe my father is sorry now too."

He drained his glass and took a step away from the fireplace. "Well, it does no one any good for us to talk about it. Anyway, I think it's time for me to put the meat on. While I do that, I'll let you set the table. I would have done it, but I looked through all the drawers in the kitchen and I couldn't turn up a tablecloth, and I couldn't locate any steak knives either."

"Oh, now I finally know what we're having for dinner," she said brightly, trying to inject a light note. She regretted having been stupid and foolish enough to mention Brad's father in the first place.

"We're having steaks; your house doesn't have a microwave, so I couldn't thaw that pizza you wanted." He slanted his head at her and smiled.

Claudia was grateful for his attempt to put things back on an even keel between them by teasing her about food. She flashed him a smile. "You said I wasn't to talk about the food until we sit down to dinner, and I shall obey your wishes."

"If you mean *all* of my wishes, that could prove highly interesting." He gave her a knowing look and lowered his voice to a whisper. "Why, before this night is over I could show you that wishes are what dreams are made of."

Claudia jumped up, pretending to ignore the innuendo in his words. She walked quickly into the dining room, took oval woven straw mats out of the buffet drawer and placed them on the table. She could feel a warm flush spreading over her neck and face, and she knew the heat was not caused by her earlier exposure to the sun. She yanked open another drawer of the buffet and withdrew two steak knives and other silverware that they would need for dinner.

"How do you like your steak cooked?" Brad called out to her.

"Medium, but a little on the rare side," she shouted back.

"Me too. See what a compatible couple we make?" She heard him add a deep chuckle to his statement. "This is already proving to be an interesting night, just as I predicted." He laughed a bit louder this time.

Claudia came back to the living room to make a comment, but Brad was on his way out the door, carrying the steaks to put them on the charcoal cooker. He was whistling one of the songs from *Oklahoma,* slightly off key but with considerable gusto. He wouldn't hear any comment she made unless she went after him and hollered at him.

Claudia picked up her cocktail glass from the table by the love seat and drank what still remained, then popped the green olive in her mouth. It was firm, and the tart, pickled taste appealed to her. A vodka martini, very dry, was proving to be a much more pleasant drink than she'd thought. It had an interesting flavor to it. She shrugged contentedly and smiled to herself. Indeed, this was proving to be an interesting night in a number of ways.

The yacht club was well filled with its usual Saturday night crowd. A bevy of spirited, noisy people were clustered around the bar, but there was a vacant table or two in a corner of the dimly lit room. As Claudia and Brad threaded their way to one of the corner tables, Claudia nodded and exchanged greetings with several people she knew, who were seated at the shallow ring of tables that bordered the dance floor. At one, a couple had just gotten up and were heading for the dance floor. Claudia spoke to them, smiling graciously.

"Nice to see you, Claudia," the attractive older woman said, but she and her husband brushed right on past them without pausing to exchange any further conversation or give Claudia an opportunity to introduce them to Brad. And the woman's expression and tone of voice belied her words. It was clearly evident that she didn't think it was at all nice to see Claudia.

"Well now, I'd say seeing you was not the high point of that couple's evening, now was it? Who are they anyway?"

"They have a place around the point from ours. They were once quite good friends with my parents."

"Once—what happened?" Brad asked, pulling out her chair for her at the table he'd found for them. "I bet you were a naughty little girl and threw rocks at their picture window." he said with a disparaging laugh. "Confess. What did you do?"

Claudia frowned and took the seat Brad offered. "I didn't do anything, but my mother did." She looked down at her hands, which were laced together and pressed firmly in her lap. "When I was in high school my mother spent a lot of time here at the lake. Lots of weekends Dad was too busy to come up with her. I haven't told you before that my mother was the kind of woman who sought attention from many men. One man's love and adoration was never enough for her. She made a play for every good-looking man up here, and that woman's husband was one of the men. That's what happened.'' She said all of this without once looking at Brad, who had by now taken his seat across the table from her.

Brad leaned toward her. "Claudia, I'm sorry," he said gently. "I shouldn't have asked."

"It was a natural question. No need to be sorry." Lifting her head, she looked at him, her sober eyes gray as dove feathers and showing not even a trace of blue.

Brad slid his hand across the table to her, turning his palm up. "Give me your hand."

She did as he asked, and he closed his fingers warmly around hers. "What are you doing this for?" she asked quietly.

"To make contact with you. Make you think about what's going on right now with you and me and not about something that took place in the past with other people." He glanced up to signal a nearby waitress but did not release her hand. "I think the waitress is coming this way. What would you like to drink?"

"Just a plain cola with lots of ice."

Brad ordered a gin and tonic, and while they waited for the girl to get their drinks for them, Claudia talked to Brad, at the same time listening with half an ear to what the small band of five musicians was playing. They were a versatile group, interspersing country and rock with some standard rhythm-and-blues numbers. When one of the players came to the microphone and began to sing a sentimental ballad in a romantic, crooning style, Brad stood up. "Come on, let's dance to that," he said, taking her hand and pulling her to her feet. They threaded their way between the tables to reach the small area cleared for dancing.

Brad put his arms around her, holding her close. They

moved together slowly in time to the music, revolving in the circle of rose-colored light, their bodies melding. When the song ended, Brad continued to hold her even though they were no longer dancing. Claudia did not move. She had no desire to break away; she enjoyed standing close to him, feeling the intimate pressure of his hand on her back and the warmth of his breath where his lips brushed her temple. He buried his nose in the silky softness of her hair. "Your hair smells good, like gardenias, roses and honeysuckle all combined. How do you manage that?" he murmured, breathing in the fragrance.

"With jasmine perfume," she whispered, laughing.

At that moment the orchestra began again, this time playing a selection in a faster tempo. Several of the less energetic couples left the floor, making room for the unrestrained dancers to enjoy the swinging rhythm.

"What do you say we show them all the right moves?" Brad said, and led her immediately into a series of turns and intricate steps as they moved together, then moved apart. Claudia and Brad danced well together, as if they'd been a team forever. She spun away from him, then came whirling back into his arms again and again, giving herself up to the excitement of the music and the joy of dancing with Brad as her partner.

Claudia was breathless when the number finished and Brad pulled her to him, first slowing their steps, then stopping altogether. They clung together now, her breast under her turquoise dress heaving from exertion and excitement. Brad too was breathing rapidly, and Claudia could feel the hard, rapid beating of his heart.

"You're a terrific dancer, Brad," she complimented him, smiling up at him with her eyes.

"Believe me, so are you!" He kept one arm circled

around her waist and started to lead her from the floor. "Let's take a breather and wait for a slow one," he said, wiping his hand across his perspiring forehead.

Back at their table, Claudia took a long drink of cola. Most of the ice in her glass had melted, leaving her drink with a weak, watered-down taste. She really didn't mind. It was cold and refreshing and that's what she needed after dancing. She put her hand to her throat and could feel that her racing pulse had finally subsided. She sensed that Brad was watching her. She glanced over at him. "What are you thinking?" she asked, aware that he was concentrating his attention solely on her.

"I was wondering what you would think if I suggested it's time we got out of here," he answered with a good-natured arch of his eyebrows.

She frowned and rubbed her index finger back and forth across her chin. "I'd think that you didn't want to dance with me anymore." Her tone was half-teasing, half-serious.

"You'd be right to a degree. I don't want to dance with you here because I find it altogether frustrating to hold you in my arms and not be able to kiss you." He leaned forward, scowling.

She parted her lips in a faint smile. "You were kissing my hair before while we were dancing."

"I want to kiss more than your hair, and you damn well know it!"

The look in his eyes made her heart skip a beat. She could feel herself growing warm under his gaze, and for a moment it seemed hard for her to breathe. He slid his hand across the table toward her as he'd done earlier. Brad's eyes held hers and something stretched between them—a feeling that quivered in the silence. Claudia placed her hand in Brad's outstretched palm. And as he clasped his strong fingers tightly around hers, she stood up. "Let's go." Her lips moved soundlessly, but Brad knew what she'd said.

They left quickly, and the minute they were in the car, Brad gathered her into his arms. The roughness of his kiss was hungry, needing, and she returned it willingly and unreservedly. His warm mouth moved over hers, his tongue touching her lips, seeking entry into her mouth. She parted her lips and their kiss was long and deep and intimate. Claudia felt the final wall of her reserve crumble; any doubts she'd harbored were forgotten. She was in love, deeply, exultingly, maturely in love with Brad, and her desire for him now triumphed over caution.

It was many moments before Brad allowed her to emerge from the warm cave of his arms. "Don't move away," he ordered, switching on the ignition. "I want to feel you beside me as I drive."

It was close to midnight, and once they were away from the club, there was scarcely any traffic. Claudia leaned her head against his shoulder and Brad took hold of her hand, holding it tightly as they drove through the night back to the house. Closing her eyes, Claudia sighed, her lips curving softly. With her hand in his she could feel the warmth flowing between them. How secure her world seemed at this moment with Brad's hand clasping hers in the darkness.

They entered at the back of the house, walking together through the kitchen to the living room. Claudia had left the lights on in the front of the house when they'd left for the yacht club. She was relieved now that she had because it made the room look normal. Everything was as usual—except for her. She was feeling strange and a little nervous. She wanted Brad to make love to her. It wasn't that she was afraid. She would never be afraid with Brad. It was a feeling of uncertainty because this was a new experience for her. It was only natural that she felt a certain hesitancy, realizing she was about to make love with a man for the first time in her life.

Assailed by these thoughts, she paused in the middle of the living room, waiting, wanting some sign from Brad.

He must have sensed her uneasiness, for he came up behind her, put his hands on her shoulders and pulled her back against him. "If I go out on the deck and smoke my pipe for a few minutes, will you take off this dress and put on something silky and blue for me to admire you in?" he asked, burying his face in the curve of her neck at the same time as he gently caressed her bare shoulders.

Claudia laughed in spite of herself.

"Hey, I didn't mean to say anything funny," he said, nuzzling the edge of her ear playfully. He turned her around so she was facing him, and he feathered a line of kisses across her forehead, ending by rubbing his nose teasingly against the tip of hers.

"You didn't really. It's only that the nightgown I brought is not blue. It's white."

"White?" His eyes narrowed slightly. "You surprise me. I thought you wore blue both day and night." Brad tilted her chin up with his hand so he could look into her eyes. "Blue or white, just don't take too long," he said, his voice betraying his emotions. He put his lips to hers and kissed her. It was a gentle kiss, but one that never lost its insistent quality. "I'm allowing you no more than fifteen minutes," he said firmly as he pushed her in the direction of her bedroom.

Claudia walked from the living room and into the

downstairs bedroom. After closing the door, she went over to the closet, took off her sundress and hung it on a hanger. As she continued to undress, she was scarcely aware of what she was doing because she felt slightly dazed from the intensity of her own emotions. It had been a long time coming, this surrender to desire.

She thought now of the men she'd known before Brad. They had been good-looking, interesting, nice men. One or two had even been rather exciting, but none had ever stirred her deeper feelings. She wanted to feel more than physical passion for a man before she gave herself to him. She wanted to feel love. And she did for Brad. He was the only one who had totally thrown her off her equilibrium, whose touch sent shivers down her spine, whose nearness made her heart race. What she felt for Brad was all-important, all-consuming emotion. She was certain of that, more certain than she'd ever been about anything in her life before.

She stepped out of her satin and lace teddy, and now with her clothes off she felt suddenly cold. She crossed her arms over her breasts, hugging herself against the chill she was experiencing. It was a warm night, and the air in the bedroom was actually extremely mild. Why was she shivering? Was she apprehensive because Brad had never said that he loved her? Her breath caught in her throat, and she swallowed hard to overcome the strange sensation she had that she was going to choke. It was true Brad had not expressed how much he cared about her in so many words, but he had shown her in other ways. He was thoughtful, attentive, and certainly his ardor went beyond mere affection. More than once she'd known the overpowering thrill of his demanding virility.

Claudia slipped her nightgown over her head. The

cloud of soft, white fabric was demurely fashioned with a full floating skirt that draped gracefully around her slender body and swirled around her feet. The bodice was overlaid with three wide bands of white lace which were threaded through with yellow satin ribbons. The ribbons tied in bows to fasten the front of the gown from the neck to the waist.

Before she tied the ribbon fastenings, Claudia applied jasmine perfume to her throat and the warm hollow between her breasts. She opened the door of the bedroom, then crossed to the dresser, picked up her brush and brushed the back and sides of her hair, fluffing it where it curled forward around her ears.

Brad's knuckles gave a token knock against the doorframe before he said, "The door is open, so I'm coming in."

The dresser was opposite the door, and Claudia could see Brad's image reflected in the mirror. He had unbuttoned the front of his shirt, pulling it loose from the waist of his trousers so it hung open, revealing his bare chest. As he started walking across the room to her, she turned around to face him.

Brad paused while his eyes made a slow trip down the length of her. "You couldn't look more beautiful even in blue," he said.

A thrill of electric excitement raced down her spine at the way he was looking at her, and her skin tingled everywhere. He continued his appraisal as if he couldn't get enough of the sight of her. When his eyes swept back to her face and locked with hers, his eyes darkened, giving a brooding intensity to his expression. "You're an angel to look at, but what you do to all my senses is not angelic, I assure you." He came to her then and touched her face, outlining her cheek with his fingers softly. "You're very beautiful, Claudia, and I know I'm not the first man to tell you that." He trailed his fingers over her throat until he came to the neck of her gown, where he pulled one end of the ribbon and untied the bow.

"But you're the one I want to have tell me. I want to be beautiful to you." There was a quiver in her voice, not only because of the state of her emotions but also because Brad had lowered his head and was kissing her neck and the hollow of her throat. In a completely involuntary movement, Claudia threw her head back so her neck was arched, fully exposed to his sensuous caress.

As Brad continued to kiss her, he loosened the second satin ribbon and allowed his hand to skim lightly across the line of her breast.

Her hand flew up and grabbed his, holding it still. "Please—"

He silenced her lips with his, kissing her with tenderness mixed with gentle urgency. Her nervous fear and resistance melted away beneath the reassuring warmth of his kiss. She freed his hand in willing surrender, curving her body into his. Brad gathered her instantly into his arms and carried her to the bed. Sitting down beside her, he untied the last ribbon bow, separating the silk and lace fabric with a caressing touch and sliding the gown off her shoulders. "How incredibly lovely you are," he exclaimed, his voice roughened by his heightened emotion. "Even more beautiful and perfect than I could have ever imagined."

Warmth rushed into her face, and she felt suddenly shy with him, uncomfortable under his gaze. "Brad—I—I want to tell you something."

He put his finger against her lips. "Shhh, darling," he whispered. He shook his head at her as he pulled his shirt off and tossed it aside. "Tell me in a minute when I'm there beside you." He quickly removed her gown, slipping it beneath her hips and down over her slender legs and feet. Without any further delay, he rid himself of his clothes and lay next to her, taking her into his arms. A quiver ran through Claudia's body, and Brad held her warmly and possessively, waiting for her to relax and grow still before he eased his embrace.

Tenderly then, he brushed her closed eyes with his lips and feathered kisses along her cheeks. He kissed the corners of her mouth and kissed her lips with teasing slowness.

"That's better. You're relaxing with me," he said, a pleased sound in his voice.

His hands roamed over her body in gentle caresses that evoked sensual stirrings in her blood. She ran her hands over the smooth skin of his back, pressing her fingers into the muscles of his shoulders. Time stood still. She was floating, drifting, lost in her feeling. She had never before experienced such depth of emotion. His mouth closed over hers and he kissed her slowly, deeply; nothing could have been stronger than the flood of emotion that continued to wash over her.

When he took his lips from hers, Claudia gave a deep sigh. "Brad, I love you so," she murmured softly.

With a low, deep-throated groan, Brad's arms closed around her with shattering strength and his body crushed her slender frame into the softness of the mattress. They held each other wordlessly. Claudia had never known anything more sensuous than the feeling of Brad's warm, bare skin against her own, touching the full length of her body, making her come alive with desire. Desire that seemed to flow from the center of her being, released by a love that was real, true and undeniable. It was a feeling that was good and right, and she responded unreservedly as Brad took her with overwhelming passion.

Chapter Eight

Claudia lay her head in the hollow of Brad's shoulder, her cheek resting against the warm wall of his chest, not stirring, not talking. She felt overwhelmed by the sheer wonder of his lovemaking—perfect, beautiful, complete. She could feel the power of him, the strength of him even as he lay still. A sensation of peace permeated every part of her. Everything was perfect; everything was right. Tears of relief rose in her eyes and spilled silently through her lashes, wetting her cheeks and making warm moist patches in the hair on Brad's chest.

"What is it, Claudia? What's the matter?" His hand was suddenly touching her cheek, wiping at her tears with his fingers. "You're crying. You're not regretting our making love, are you?" There was distress and concern in his voice.

"No, don't think that," she answered, moving her head against his chest in denial.

"But what have I done?"

She curved her body even closer. "You've made me happy, wonderfully happy. That's why I'm crying."

"I—don't understand. If I made you happy, why are you crying?" He hugged her to him, pressing his lips against the soft strands of her hair where it fell over her forehead.

"Because I feel so relieved. I know now that I never, never will be like my mother. I could never have careless encounters or a series of meaningless affairs. I never really thought I might, but now I've proved it in my own mind. I've proved it with you." She sighed softly. "I waited—waited until I knew for sure that I was in love. It was the only way it could be right for me. You see, Brad, I've never made love with anyone before."

Brad's body shuddered against hers, and he drew in his breath sharply. "I realized that, Claudia. I think I sensed it all along. That's why I stopped you when you tried to tell me." He said the words flatly, as if he were talking to himself, not to her.

Claudia felt the hard, erratic beating of his heart against her cheek. She wanted Brad to say something more to her, something caring, but he didn't. She could feel how tense his body had become, but he lay perfectly still, one arm around her shoulders, his now shallow, uneven breathing making a warm stirring at the edge of her hair. She didn't know what she expected, but Brad's reaction confused her. Didn't it matter to him that he was the first lover she'd ever known?

As quickly as the thought came, she pushed it aside. Of course it mattered to him; she told herself. And it was because it was important to his feelings about her that he didn't talk about it to her yet. Her lips parted in a smile and, eased by her own rationalizing, she shut her eyes, content now to go to sleep in Brad's arms.

Brad's mind whirled in torment, appalled at what he'd done. Had his determination to wreak revenge on Howard Carlton blinded him to Claudia's vulnerability? Had he refused to consider the ramifications of his actions just to even the score between a Hayes and a Carlton? My God! He didn't want to hurt Claudia. He cared about her. Certainly he could never deny that fact. He clenched his teeth and fought against the riptide of emotions that forced him to examine his motivations for everything he'd done.

Forcing himself to lie still, he tried to make his mind go blank while he waited for Claudia to fall asleep, but he found it impossible. He couldn't stop his memory's vivid replay of the night he'd met Howard Carlton. All through that evening at the Tulsa Club, Howard had made it blatantly obvious that he didn't want Claudia involved other than in a strictly business way with the son of Sam Hayes. Indeed, he resented Brad's attention to his daughter. Howard had made that clearly apparent.

Brad's forehead knotted in an intense frown. Had realizing how much Howard feared the developing relationship between them added impetus to Brad's pursuit of Claudia? A twinge of guilt made his temples throb with jackhammer persistence.

Brad felt as if his nerves were screaming, and then suddenly the pressure inside him lessened slightly as Claudia's breathing took on the deep, even pattern of sleep. With infinite care, Brad eased her head onto the pillow, and then with slow, careful movements he moved his body away from hers and slid out of bed.

Brad paused long enough to pull on his pants, then

slung his shirt over one shoulder and left the room. He didn't stop in the living room, nor did he head toward the stairs leading up to the bedrooms in the loft. He strode purposefully outside, walking the length of the deck. For a while he stood, his hands leaning on the redwood railing, and stared out through the dark trees toward the even darker water of the lake. There was a slender slice of a moon, which sent out only a token light in the sky. There were stars, but their radiance too seemed dim, as if tonight they lacked the power to shine from such a distance.

Because he didn't know what else to do with it, he put on his shirt, fastening the three lower buttons. He didn't need to wear it because the night was mild, more like a July night than June. But tucking the shirttail into the waist of his slacks and rolling up the sleeves to just above his elbows occupied his hands and thoughts for a minute or so. Something so mundane was a welcome respite from his other, plaguing thoughts. He started to sit down in one of the canvas deck chairs, then changed his mind. He crossed the deck, sat down on the top step and, propping his elbows on his knees, rested his chin in his hands.

Staring unseeingly into the black void of the night, Brad thought about all that had happened since fate had decreed his meeting with Claudia that afternoon at the well site. From the moment she'd told him her name, had he ever really thought of her in any other way than as the daughter of the man who had harmed his parents? He cleared his throat in a hoarse growl. Surely he had. And from that first time he'd laid eyes on her, she'd never been far from his mind. He'd seen how lovely, vibrant and exciting she was that first day in her office. And at lunch afterward, hadn't he felt the strong attraction that was already rampant between them? She was so appealing that he could scarcely keep his hands off her, and he'd decided at that moment, when the wind tousled her golden hair across her lovely face, that she was the most beautiful creature he'd ever seen. He willingly admitted the intensity of the desire he'd felt for her from the beginning. Why was he suddenly assailed with self-recriminations? Involuntarily his hand gripped his chin in a vise. What made him suddenly feel compelled to question his own motivations?

Brad buried his head in his hands. He'd said she was special. Now he knew just how special Claudia Carlton actually was. She was trusting, caring, loving and giving. And she was vulnerable, much too vulnerable.

He hunched his shoulders in a gesture of despair. He was going to have to come up with some explanation for ignoring her vulnerability, for treating her as a practiced lover. He owed Claudia that. He owed her the truth. But at the moment he was damned if he knew just what the truth was!

The velvet darkness of night faded into the soft gray that precedes the first pink shade of sunrise. Claudia stirred, rolled over on her side and reached out toward Brad only to discover he was gone. His side of the bed had smooth cool sheets. There was no warm impression to indicate that his departure was a recent one.

Claudia experienced a twinge of regret that he had left the bed ahead of her. In her mind, she had visualized awakening and finding him still sleeping beside her. Then she could have touched his cheek, brushed her fingers over the rusty red stubble of his morning growth of beard. The idea was so appealing that she rolled over to his side of the bed, burying her face in his pillow where his head had lain. Drawing in her breath slowly, she imagined that the clean scent of his hair and the male scent of his body still clung to the bed linen. She pulled the sheet up to her face, enveloping herself in his very essence.

Claudia lay there for several long moments, remembering the ultimate happiness his lovemaking had brought her. She thought too of how afterward Brad had held her close in his arms and she had fallen asleep with his lips pressed against her temple, his warm breath soft in her hair. Her recollections brought a smile. She reached up now, touching a single soft curl as if within it she might discover a caress, a lingering trace of Brad's infinite tenderness.

The room had grown a degree lighter. She sat up, reaching for her nightgown so she could go looking for Brad. It occurred to her to be a trifle curious. Why had Brad gotten up before it was even morning? Where had he gone? What would he be doing in these predawn hours instead of sleeping?

Apprehension like bony fingers seemed suddenly to be closing around her heart. Instead of going out into the living room, she ran barefoot across the deep-piled carpet to the window of the bedroom, which looked out to the deck. Leaning her head close to the glass, she peered out into the rose-streaked dawn.

She saw Brad sitting on the top step, his back propped against the post of the railing that surrounded the deck. He was sitting sideways, but his face was toward the house. In the pale morning light, his face appeared drawn with lines of fatigue as if he hadn't slept all night. His long arms were draped loosely across his chest, and he appeared totally absorbed in thought.

Claudia stared at Brad in a kind of tortured fascination. She felt as if she could not draw her eyes away from his telltale expression. It was as if she were hypnotized by the look of pained regret written in every line of Brad's face. There might as well have been words written there for her to read, so clearly was it spelled out to her now the reason Brad had for leaving her alone in her bed. He regretted what had happened between them. And since he did, the reason was undeniably clear to Claudia. Brad had never intended a serious or lasting commitment to her, and her declaration of love had placed an unwanted burden on him. One he now had to find a way to extricate himself from.

Claudia began to tremble all over as the pain of her anguished emotions engulfed her. She turned away from the window and the sight of Brad and walked to the center of the room. She stood there a long time, her face buried in her hands as she wept silently.

It took awhile for her to emerge from the torment of her thoughts and resign herself to all that had come to pass. Finally she raised her head and took a determined step toward the bathroom. She would shower, she would get dressed and she would handle the disenchantment of the day. After all, she had known the splendor of the night.

Brad obviously had heard her taking her shower and moving around as she got dressed. Now she could hear the noise of the water in the pipes and she knew he was showering in the bathroom in the loft.

She began to hurry because she wanted to be dressed and in the kitchen fixing breakfast before Brad came downstairs. Hastily tugging a pink tee shirt over her head, she thought that, no matter what, Brad must not come into the bedroom looking for her.

She had rumpled her hair pulling on the shirt, so she smoothed it with her hairbrush. As she did, she looked at her reflection in the dresser mirror. How pale she was, and the strawberry pink shorts and shirt simply drew attention to her palor. Quickly she applied blusher to her cheeks and a rose red lipstick to her lips.

She had orange juice poured, sweet rolls in the oven warming, and was just placing three strips of bacon in a frying pan when Brad came downstairs from the loft. He had showered and shaved and was wearing fresh khaki pants and a beige pullover shirt, the perfect complement to his burnished copper hair and rich earth-colored eyes. He entered the kitchen with a smile. Only the web of lines that feathered the corners of his eyes and the dark circles beneath them betrayed his troubled state of mind.

"Say, you're taking over my job as chief cook around here. I can't allow that." His light, bright tone sounded too hearty. She sensed he was making a determined effort to have everything appear perfectly normal between them.

"First one in the kitchen starts breakfast. That's a house rule here," she countered with forced gaiety.

"I'm here now, so I'll take over." Brad joined her in front of the range, taking the long-handled fork that she'd been using to turn the bacon. Then he nodded in the direction of the tall stools that were tucked under the kitchen bar. "Sit down and drink your juice. I'll fry you two eggs, over easy."

"No eggs for me, or bacon either. I've a sweet roll heating in the oven."

"That's hardly what I'd call a hearty breakfast."

Claudia shrugged but didn't comment.

"You should have bacon and eggs too, to keep your strength up. I expect strong-armed help with the sailing today." He opened the carton of eggs and set it on the counter next to the stove.

"A roll is all I want, Brad," she snapped.

Hearing the sharp edge to her voice, he eyed her

quizzically. He responded with a constrained, "Okay, honey. One sweet roll it is."

Claudia didn't look at him, but she did jump off the stool and go open the oven. She took out one of the two rolls she'd been warming and put it on a plate, then returned to perch on her stool.

Brad broke two eggs into the frying pan. "I guess I just learned something else about your eating habits. You don't indulge in large breakfasts. Well, that's all right. I'll just fix an extra large picnic lunch for us to take sailing. You'll discover you've got a he-man appetite after we've been out on the lake for a few hours." He chattered glibly to her as he sprinkled salt and pepper on his eggs and rummaged through a drawer under the kitchen counter until he located a spatula.

"We're not going sailing today."

"Oh?" There was a questioning inflection in Brad's voice. "So what are we going to do? Go fishing, swimming?"

Claudia had been eating pecan-filled bites of the caramel-covered roll. She wiped sweet syrup from the corner of her mouth before she answered. "I want to go back to Tulsa as soon as we've eaten breakfast," she stated flatly.

Brad spun around sharply to face her, his back now to the stove. "You're kidding, aren't you?"

"No, I mean it."

"Why?" He stared at her, obviously perturbed. "We'd planned to stay over today and drive back early in the morning, I thought."

Claudia could feel the tension building up inside her. She pressed her lips together so tightly they whitened as she raised her chin and looked over at Brad. "I want to drive back today."

Brad frowned in deep perplexity as he studied her. "If you're worried about our making it back to Tulsa tomorrow morning in time for you to get to work, then we'll drive back after dinner tonight. I can think of no reason for us to leave before that." He turned abruptly back to the stove, served up his bacon and eggs on a plate and pushed the frying pan onto one of the unused burners away from the heat. Then he came over and took his place on the stool next to Claudia's.

"I can think of several reasons," she said, her voice trembling because his nearness was having an unsettling effect on her nerves. It had been difficult enough talking to him when he was standing at the stove a few feet away, but now that he was sitting right next to her, so close that their shoulders were almost touching and she could smell the light, clean scent of his after-shave, she doubted if she could carry through. She felt like a rubber band that had been stretched too far and too thin. "Brad," she said quietly, praying that she could conceal from him the extent of her emotional damage, "you see, I saw you sitting out there on the deck before daybreak. I believe you were doing what I now need to do."

Brad had picked up a piece of his bacon. Now he dropped it back on his plate. "What do you mean, Claudia?" A quiver of emotion ran over Brad's strong face; the sight of it made Claudia's breath catch.

Her hand automatically moved up to cover her throat. She swallowed hard. "We both know that the quiet hours between midnight and dawn are a time for sorting out things in our lives. Weren't you doing that? Isn't that the reason you left my bedroom?"

His body tensed. "Something like that," he answered grimly. A worried frown knotted his brow, and as he looked at her, the light seemed to fade from his eyes so that instead of a rich brown they were now the drab color of dead leaves. "I want to talk to you today. I need to explain something. I have to ex—"

"No," she cried out, interrupting him. "You don't have to explain anything. I'm sure I already understand." She kept shaking her head as she said this to him, wanting to make it clear that she didn't want him to talk about any aspect of last night with her now.

"You don't understand, Claudia." He raised his voice, grabbing hold of her arm where it lay on the bar between her plate and his. "How could you, when I'm not altogether sure I do myself?"

She couldn't draw her eyes away from his face. Wordlessly she took in the deep lines next to his mouth, the strained twist of his lips. She tried to pull her arm from beneath his hand, but he tightened his grasp, his fingers bruising her tender skin. "We have to spend this day out there on the water, sailing and talking," he said, an insistent sharpness in his tone of voice. "I need to tell you something. I know I owe you some explanations, but they're neither simple nor easy to tell in a way that you'll understand. The place for us to talk about all of this is in the sailboat." He leaned his face closer to hers. "Things are right between us when we're handling a boat together." The grim lines of his mouth eased.

She looked away. What possible explanation did he think he could offer her that she didn't already know? Even if he thought he had one, wouldn't it only hurt her more? He was incapable of feeling the love for her that she felt for him. That was the simple fact of it all. She understood that, and it was all she could possibly bear to know.

She took a deep breath, pressing back tears. The tightness she had been feeling across her shoulders had increased until it was now a vicious ache all across her back. This had to end. She couldn't handle herself with Brad for much longer. She mustn't break down. She mustn't allow him to know how much he'd hurt her. She'd given him everything else; she prayed silently now that she could save some shred of her pride, keep some semblance of dignity.

Sliding off her stool, she pulled her hand from his grasp. A misty sheen of tears filmed her eyes. She turned her back quickly so Brad would not see how distressed she was. She walked to the kitchen window and looked out.

"It's impossible, Brad. This is not a day for us to either talk or sail. No one who's wise would go out on the lake today. Just look at the sky. There are such dark clouds against the sun." Her voice caught in a harsh, strangled sound. Without glancing back at him, she walked purposefully out of the kitchen to pack her things and then close up the house so they could leave.

Outwardly at least, Claudia had managed to draw the curtain across the stage of her personal relations with Brad, but she still had to carry out the El-Sa lease with him. On Monday morning she took the El-Sa contracts to her father.

"When you've signed these, leave them with Myra. Brad Hayes will be here later today to add his signature and pick up his copy."

Howard cleared the space in front of him on his desk, making room for the contracts. "I take it then that Brad is coming back in town today."

"He came in Friday," she said, moving restlessly

around the room. "He took me to Discoveryland." She stopped in front of the mahogany bookshelves at one side of Howard's office and nervously fingered the rows of neatly aligned books.

Howard cleared his throat noisily. "I hope you're not letting yourself get seriously involved with Brad." Howard's blue eyes now took on a troubled expression. "Are you?" His voice was concerned and gentle.

He's worried about me, she thought, and the realization touched her. "I was, but that's changed now." She managed to give him a tight smile. "And now with the lease contracts signed and ready to deliver, I won't have any more dealings with him." She was glad that her voice sounded steady and normal. She hoped to hide from her father her true feelings for Brad.

Howard gripped his chin between his thumb and forefinger and angled his head at her in an approving manner. "I'm damn relieved to hear that. I don't mind telling you I am. I admit the whole thing bothered me from the start. The water is just too blasted muddy between the Hayeses and the Carltons to ever run clear again. And human nature being what it is, I was afraid they might attempt to even the score using you."

Claudia reeled as if she'd been struck. She leaned against the bookshelves to steady herself. It wasn't possible. Was it? All the color drained from her face. She remembered the words Brad had said to her. "I owe you some explanations, but they're neither simple nor easy to tell." It was as if she were hearing him say them again right at that moment, for the words repeated and repeated like a stuck phonograph record playing in her ear.

"Sam couldn't get back at me through the business. My company is solid, always has been." Her father's deep voice reached her through the agony of her thoughts, forcing her to realize he was still theorizing about Brad's motives and Sam's. "He never had the means or the power to get revenge on me financially, but he did personally." Howard's voice hardened and everything about him was tense, his shoulders, the set of his mouth and the strained, tortured look in the depths of his eyes. "Yeah, Sam Hayes has seen more than once how vulnerable I am when someone I love is involved. And Claudia, you're the one thing that means more to me than this company."

Claudia had not seen her father this emotional since her mother's death. Howard got up out of his chair, and she came to him and threw her arms around his neck and hugged him. It was a rare moment between them. Claudia didn't say anything; she simply hugged him for a moment.

When she left her father's office a few minutes later, she stopped at Myra's desk only long enough to tell her about the El-Sa contracts she had left with her father.

"Brad Hayes will be in some time later today, so if you can have him sign them and give him his copy, I'd appreciate it," she explained, talking rapidly as if she were in a rush to get back to her own office.

"Don't you want me to return the contracts to you, let you handle these final details with Brad Hayes yourself?" Myra inquired with a smile.

"No."

Myra's eyes flared in surprise. Realizing how terse she had sounded, Claudia apologized. "I sound uptight and I'm sorry. The truth is I don't want to see Brad. I won't be here anyway. I've got an appointment with a land

man over at Phillips Petroleum. I'm driving to Bartlesville in time for lunch, and I won't be coming back to the
office.''

"May I explain that to Brad?"

"If he asks. But I doubt if he will." Claudia shrugged
and headed for the elevator.

Chapter Nine

Claudia felt as if she'd accomplished a major feat, and indeed she had. Once she left her father's office that morning she had managed to put all thought of Brad on hold at the back of her mind and concentrate totally on the work she needed to accomplish. She was determined to keep her emotional upheaval from affecting her career. Maintaining a well-disciplined mind where business was concerned was a trait she'd inherited from her father. She took pride in it.

Driving back to Tulsa from Bartlesville, however, the disquieting possibilities her father had mentioned festered in her mind. Had she deluded herself from the beginning, believing that Brad at least cared a little about her? She hated to think she could have been so big a fool.

By the time she reached her apartment she had worked herself into a highly emotional state. One that made her completely unprepared to see Brad's car parked directly in front of the walk to her door. Yet there he was. And before she had wheeled her car up to the curb, Brad was out of his car, waiting for her to park and turn off the motor. As soon as she did, he flung open the door on the driver's side so she could get out.

"I've been here waiting for you since five o'clock. Are you just getting back from Bartlesville?" His brown eyes peered at her anxiously.

"How did you know I was in Bartlesville?"

"I asked where you were when I didn't find you in your office. I was worried that you were trying to avoid me." He smiled wryly. "You weren't, were you?"

"I was working." She made it a flat statement and did not elaborate. She got out of the car and pushed the button that locked the car doors, then moved to allow Brad to close the door after her.

"I want to take you out someplace for dinner."

She brushed past him, starting up the walk to her apartment. "I've eaten," she said when he caught up to her. "I stopped at a cafeteria at one of the shopping malls."

"I'm sorry. I was counting on taking you out."

It was such a mundane conversation for them to be having. She frowned slightly, wanting somehow to escape from him. "Since you haven't eaten and I have, you go along. Get yourself some dinner."

"I can wait, Claudia." He put his hand under her elbow, hurrying her along the walk. "Right now you and I must talk."

"You did find the contracts in order. You were satisfied, weren't you?"

"Yes. They were okay."

"And you signed them then?"

"Claudia, I said the contracts were fine. And you know

very well I didn't wait here for two hours to tell you that I signed the darn contracts."

"No, you waited here for two hours to ask to take me to dinner," she countered with a slight smile that for a moment at least eased the tension between them.

"Hey, that's better." He smiled for the first time, tightening his hold on her arm, pulling her against his side so that his body brushed the side of hers as they walked.

She stopped, pulling immediately away from him and quickly opening her purse to get out her door key. She unlocked her apartment door but didn't open it. Instead she stood with her hand on the polished brass doorknob, looking back over her shoulder at him. "Was there something else, Brad?"

"Stop it!" He raised his voice in anger. "You know damn well there's something else. There's everything else." His eyes blazed, their color changing from brown to glittering jet black. "Now you open that door and go inside. We can't talk out here on your doorstep."

Claudia raised her chin to him at a defiant angle. "We can for what I have to say," she said with a cool tone that sounded so calm and controlled it surprised her. "And that's good night."

"You're not putting me off this time, Claudia. You refused to discuss this with me Sunday morning at the lake, and I didn't press you then. But I have to go back to Texas tomorrow morning, and I've no intention of leaving here tonight until you and I have reached an understanding about our relationship." With that, he planted his hand over hers, turning the doorknob and pushing open the door to her apartment. "After you," he said with exaggerated politeness, his expression implacable. He moved back then, waiting for her to precede him through the open doorway.

As she entered, Brad followed closely behind her and walked with her into the living room. Turning on first one lamp then another, Claudia was aware of how their two shadows touched, forming a velvet pattern on the living room wall. It unnerved her that he continued to stay so close to her now that they were inside the apartment.

"I wish you'd just sit down and not follow me around," she said bluntly.

"Okay, where do you prefer *we* sit?" he acquiesced, sounding amused.

"*You* sit anywhere in the living room that you like. I'm going in the kitchen to see what I can find for you to eat."

"I don't want you to. Please don't bother."

"You haven't had dinner and I know you're hungry." She went into the kitchen and opened the refrigerator. "How about two ham and cheese sandwiches on rye bread? It's the best I can offer."

"Plenty good enough. Thanks, I'd like that." There was a pause, then he called out to her, "You wouldn't happen to have a cold beer to go with that, would you?"

"I would not," she shouted back, showing a tinge of irritation. "You'll have to settle for coffee, tea or milk."

"Coffee then, but only if you'll have it with me."

She got out the coffee pot, measured water and coffee and plugged in the cord. In rapid order she took ham, cheese, mayonnaise and lettuce from the refrigerator and, opening a loaf of rye bread, began to prepare Brad's food. Though he did not come near the kitchen, she knew that he wasn't sitting down as she'd suggested. She could hear him moving restlessly around the living room.

Ten minutes later, however, when she came in bringing his sandwiches on a tray with two cups of coffee, he was sitting near the center of the sofa, leafing casually through a recent copy of the *Oil and Gas Journal*. As she set the tray down on the coffee table in front of him, he immediately closed the magazine and set it aside.

"This looks good," he said, grabbing up one of the sandwiches and biting into it with gusto.

Claudia took her cup and saucer and sat down in the nearby wing chair.

"I was hungry. This tastes great," he found time to mumble in the brief period between swallowing one bite and taking another.

"Not as great as one of your submarine sandwiches, I bet." She laughed softly.

Brad's brown eyes glanced warmly over to her face, remaining there long enough to seem to caress every feature. He said nothing, only narrowed one eye finally in a slight wink, as if to indicate they were both sharing the same memory about a submarine sandwich. With that, he returned to his eating.

Claudia leaned back into the sheltering wing of the high-backed chair. She studied the level of the brown liquid in her cup before taking another sip. She kept her eyes lowered, willing herself to relax. Brad was going to force her to hear him out. There was no way she could escape that now. She had never had more ambivalent feelings about anything in her life than she did about this. She was actually afraid to hear the explanations Brad felt were so important to tell her, yet she was curious about them too. What woman in love wouldn't be? Feeling the hard pulsing in the base of her throat, she wondered how she'd manage to get through the next half hour with him. And if she did, would she be happier? Would she then have some small hope that Brad would come to love her as she did him? Or would she then have no hope at all?

Brad was halfway through the second sandwich. He reached over and took his cup of coffee off the tray, taking a swallow before setting it down next to his plate. "I had an interesting talk with Myra Allan this afternoon," he commented, picking up the remaining portion of his food.

Claudia looked over at him, dumbfounded. Brad's mentioning Myra was the last thing she would have expected. "You—you did? That's—good," she stammered, frowning because she wondered what reason Brad might have for leading off their conversation in this way. He was usually so direct. Was he now going to try some subtle type of subterfuge? She wasn't going to like it if he did.

"I told her I'd mentioned meeting her to Sam and that he certainly remembered the pretty young girl who worked for Howard some twenty years ago. My dad's an Irishman who always could beguile a woman with his blarney."

"Like father, like son," she teased, fingering the tiny cleft in her chin.

He shrugged and continued with what he was saying. "The interesting thing I learned is that Myra really did know Dad pretty well. She had a couple of anecdotes about him and your father that I enjoyed hearing."

Claudia shot him a quizzical look. "Myra did?" Her voice was disbelieving. She was remembering how vague Myra had been the afternoon when she'd questioned her about El-Sa and Sam Hayes. Myra had acted as if she could scarcely recall the name. And the day they had lunch together, Myra had been reticent to say much. Why would Myra hold back knowledge about Brad's father from her? Both Myra and her father had been trying hard to keep something from her, it seemed. "I guess I was wrong. I had the idea Myra didn't know Sam all that well."

"She not only knew him, but she told me she admired

him because he was a man with an indomitable spirit." Brad had finished eating and was brushing his hands together, dusting off crumbs of the rye bread. "It made me feel good hearing her say that. She's right about Dad too. Old Copperhead never gives up and never gives in."

Claudia stood up, carrying her cup and saucer over to the coffee table. "Can I get you more coffee?"

"I'll just finish this," he said, shaking his head.

"Do you want something else to eat? I could get you a bowl of ice cream. Maybe scrape up some store-bought cookies?"

"I don't want anything else. This was fine." He waved his hand over his empty plate. "What I want is for you to sit here on the sofa with me so we can talk."

Claudia complied and sat down at the end of the sofa away from him, tucking her legs up under her and smoothing her skirt over her knees. "Why were you telling me all this about Myra?" She pursed her lips, tapping her index finger against them thoughtfully. "I'm sure you have some reason for it."

He angled his body so that he was facing her. "Today I had the feeling that Myra knows a great deal more about both my father and yours than we could imagine. That she could tell me what I've always wanted to know: the reason why your father had to do what he did to Sam all those years ago."

If Brad was suppressing anger as well as his dislike of Howard, he did it well. His well-modulated voice was both low and calm. "Why didn't you just ask her?" Claudia asked, making her voice as carefully mild as his.

"I didn't have the opportunity. A couple of men came into the office about that time. She had to do something for them. Since I'd already taken care of the lease contracts, I had no further excuse to hang around. I have my doubts that she would have given me the details I want to learn anyway. I'm the outsider at Carlton Petroleum, after all.'' He shrugged, but continued to look at Claudia.

She smiled faintly, arching her brows. ''Is this your subtle way of getting me to ask Myra for you?''

He returned her smile. ''It did occur to me that you might talk to her.''

''Believe me, I've already tried. A couple of times, in fact.'' She ran her hands mindlessly over the smooth fabric of her skirt as she spoke. ''She won't talk to me about the trouble Dad caused for your father. Myra says, like you, that she's an outsider. That my dad has to be the one to tell me. If he wants me to know, that is. From the way she put it, I got the distinct idea that he may not want me to know.'' She quieted her hands by interlacing her fingers.

''I'll buy that.'' Brad's sarcasm was only lightly veiled. ''Why would he want to tell you the reasons for what he did when he never saw fit to tell Sam? My God, Claudia, do you see how unfair it's all been? Your father deliberately set out to destroy a man's business. He ruined my dad, broke him financially and never, mind you, never once gave him a single reason for doing what he did.'' Brad's calm voice and mild manner had vanished abruptly. He regarded her now with eyes that had grown fierce with resentment.

Claudia stared at him. She'd never seen Brad worked up like this before. He'd been bitter the times he'd told her about having to move from Tulsa. He harbored strong animosity toward Howard for what he'd done, but Brad had never revealed as clearly as he was doing tonight how deeply ingrained in the fiber of his life it all was.

''You can bet your life your father doesn't want you to know what it was that made him forsake principles of human decency and his own personal integrity. And that's what he did in order to ruin Sam. Did you know that?''

She pressed her hand to her brow, looking at Brad with troubled eyes. ''I know he ended the verbal contract he'd had with your father, and that shocked me. I wouldn't have believed my father would do such a thing. But that's all in the past, and it's their past, not ours.'' She began shaking her head as if to negate what was over and done. ''Honestly, Brad, let's talk about something else. Surely you didn't force your way in here tonight to get me to speculate with you about the reasons why my father and yours ended their business relations all those years ago.'' Experiencing a twinge of apprehension, Claudia crossed her arms across her chest, hugging herself as if she could ward off a hurting blow. ''You're building up to something else, aren't you?''

''I'm pointing out the reason why it seemed like fate when Howard Carlton's daughter contacted El-Sa concerning a lease contract. I enjoyed the irony of the fact that Sam Hayes now had something that Howard Carlton wanted. I was plenty curious to find out how badly you might want what we had.''

''You and your father didn't act curious. You ignored my letter and phone calls for weeks.''

Some of his angry tension seemed to dissipate, and he leaned back against the thick cushions of the sofa, stretching his legs out straight and crossing his feet at his ankles. ''Well, naturally Dad didn't want to get involved with Carlton Petroleum ever again. It took some arguing to convince him to let me have a go with it. But the way I looked at it, I had nothing to lose and maybe I could make a deal that would give me a bit of satisifaction.''

''You felt vindictive?''

''Wouldn't you have in my place?'' he challenged.

"Probably." Claudia's eyes were thoughtful. "I don't know."

"I can tell you that I think you would. It's only human nature to want retribution."

She caught her breath at his words, then let it out slowly. "Someone else said that very same thing to me just this morning." Shifting her position, she untucked her leg from under her. "That's why you made things so hard for me that first day in my office. I was Howard Carlton's daughter, so you decided to make it rough. Do you remember how you argued, haggled and beat me down over every detail? You made me explain things you already knew fully, and you tried to confuse me by bringing up aspects that had no bearing on what we were talking about."

"I did lay it on, but you were an able sparring partner."

"Was I?" She laughed disparagingly. "I didn't feel like it. You had me so confused, I felt as if I were contending with the most difficult business arrangement I'd ever dealt with. If we hadn't stopped to go to lunch, I'd have bet that you'd never have come to terms with me on that lease."

Brad had inched closer to her as she spoke. Now he stretched his arm across the back of the sofa behind her and let his fingers brush gently over the nape of her neck. His touch was tentative and yet it affected her powerfully. It was the first gesture of affection he'd made toward her tonight. "Over lunch I did see what an appealing creature you were, I admit," he teased.

"And then and there you got a sudden attack of conscience. Am I right?"

His fingers idled and then he withdrew his hand. "No, that came later," he said tonelessly.

In an involuntary gesture, her hand moved to her face

and she pressed her cool fingers against her lips. Did he mean what she thought he did? Was he admitting that his attack of conscience had come after they made love together at the lake house? She looked at him. It seemed that her father was right. A river of muddy water never can run clear. For even when the dirt begins to settle to the bottom of the riverbed, along comes a heavy rain which washes in more silt. The analogy was apt. With every word, Brad was forcing her to see how apt it actually was.

"You needn't have bothered your conscience about me at all." Claudia said as she jumped to her feet and walked over to the fireplace. Keeping her back carefully toward Brad, she pushed at the base of one of the brass candlesticks, positioning it farther away from the clock. "One way or another you accomplished what you wanted in the business deal between us," she said, continuing to talk to him without turning around. "I'm sure both you and your father know that fifteen hundred dollars an acre is twice what the company paid for any other lease in Stephens County. El-Sa got the best of this deal with Carlton. That should give both you and Sam personal as well as financial satisfaction." Her words rang out in the quiet room, revealing the tension and anger she was trying to keep from him by not letting him see her face. "Now for heaven's sake, let's not rehash this further. The contracts are signed and the deal is closed between Carlton and Alamo Drilling."

"And what about between you and me?"

Hearing his words, she felt like a coiled spring with no room to expand. She whirled around as anger exploded inside her. "I'll bite. You tell me what can possibly be between two people, one named Hayes and one named Carlton." She stood there, her shoulders tense and her cold eyes glittering like blue ice. "Nothing but vindictive feelings. Isn't that right? Isn't that what you said?"

Brad got up from the sofa and crossed to her, frowning in concern. When he reached her, he put both hands on her arms. "I said between us, you and me, Claudia. I'm not talking about feelings that exist between Sam and Howard. Let's leave our fathers out of this and talk strictly about you and me."

"Can you do that?" she asked in a clipped tone. "I don't think you can." She broke away from his light hold, walking around him to pace back across the carpeted floor.

"What makes you think that?"

"Because I don't believe I exist for you except as Howard Carlton's daughter."

"That's ridiculous."

"Is it?" Her anger was fanned into high flame now, and she whirled when she reached the middle of the room, throwing her chin up as she planted both hands on her hips. "You can't deny that you knew it would upset my father if you and I became involved, can you?"

Brad leveled his troubled gaze on her. "I'd say he made that fact clear the night he took us to dinner. I could hardly say his attitude came as a surprise to me either, if that's what you mean. But it isn't, is it?" An expression of pain contorted his features.

She could actually see the color drain from his face as he took a step toward her, his hand outstretched, entreating. "Don't say anything more. You've made your point." He drew his hand back, letting his arm fall to his side. "You've also answered my question. Between you and me are insurmountable odds." His eyes remained locked on hers a few seconds longer; then without saying anything further, he moved slowly past her, not stopping until the reached the door. With his hand on the doorknob, he hesitated, looking back at her over his shoulder.

"I'll be seeing you, Claudia," he said tonelessly.

She wondered if he'd said this because he found it easier than to say good-bye. She nodded her head in response but didn't utter a sound. She felt unable to force a single word through her trembling lips.

The door opened and closed quickly and Brad was gone. Claudia didn't see him leave because she was blinded by the tears that fell freely from her sad eyes— tears that could not be controlled.

Chapter Ten

In Oklahoma not all June winds are gentle and not all June days are fair, but Claudia felt relieved that for the next two weeks there was only sunshine. If there had been days when gray clouds hid the sun, she'd have been reminded of that Sunday at the lake with Brad. And if there had been numerous days of rain, which often occurs this time of year, she probably would have viewed the rain as tears of sorrow come to wash away the memory of lost love. At least that seemed to be her mood since Brad had gone back to Texas.

She had not heard a word from him, and it was unlikely now that she would. He'd found a way to ease himself out of a difficult situation, and that obviously was exactly what he had intended doing. Time and distance take care of a lot of things. The thought was irritating, leaving a bitter taste in her mouth.

The phone was ringing as she entered her apartment Friday evening. She hurried down the hall and picked up the extension in her bedroom. "Hello," she said, sounding slightly breathless.

"You sound like you ran to get the phone. I know you must have just gotten in because I've been calling every fifteen minutes since five o'clock. It's me, Brad," he explained unnecessarily, for there was no way she wouldn't recognize his voice. "I was determined to reach you, persistent Capricorn, remember."

"Uh-huh," she mumbled, still adjusting her mind to the surprise of hearing his voice.

"How have you been? What have you been doing?"

"Busy and working." She paused, taking a deep breath to slow her racing heart and steady her voice. "Now that we have the leases we need, plans are going ahead for the Stephens area." She threw their business out at him, knowing it was a safer subject between them than anything personal would be.

"Does it look like you'll start drilling before the summer is out?"

"Possibly. We'll be in a position to know in another week or ten days."

"That's one of the reasons I called. In case you come to a decision and need to reach me, I wanted to let you know I'll be in Canada. I'm going to Calgary on some business for the oil well supply end of El-Sa."

Claudia twisted her fingers absently in the plastic coils of the telephone cord. Why, she wondered, did Brad feel it was necessary to explain his business plans to her? "No problem there," she said, shrugging. "If and when there's a decision, I can talk to your father. After all, he's Alamo Drilling."

"I want you to talk to me," Brad said, raising his voice. "And you darn well know I do," he persisted stubbornly.

She cringed, assailed by a sudden, unsettling thought. Was it possible that Brad was saying this because he knew his father would not wish to talk to her? Must she keep all business dealings strictly between herself and Brad for the reason that Sam Hayes wanted nothing to do with the daughter of Howard Carlton? Shaken by this, she stretched the phone cord across the night stand in order to be able to sit on the chaise longue a few feet from the bed.

"It's unlikely I'll be calling anyway. The company's production man will be in charge when it comes to actual drilling," she said in a matter-of-fact tone which belied the uneasiness she was feeling. The idea that Brad's father disliked her without even knowing her was making her feel more defensive by the minute: "Honestly, Brad, this is rather a pointless conversation for a Friday night. You could have called me at the office on Monday to tell me you were going to Canada, and to tell you the truth, it would have been better if you had."

"I know I could have called the office Monday, but the truth is you were on my mind and I wanted to talk to you now. You can't blame me for not waiting when I wanted to hear your voice tonight, can you?"

Her fingers tightened around the telephone. Why was he saying this? Was he trying to hurt her further? Didn't he know that a warm, tender, caring word from him destroyed the protective defenses she was struggling so hard to maintain? "No—no, I can't blame you—not for anything," she said in a choked voice. "It would be far easier for me if I could. Good-bye, Brad," she said quickly, and hung up. Trembling, she sat there for a time, her hand resting on the silent phone. She thought about her feelings for Brad, analyzed them, dissected them one by one, then put them back in order again. The results were the same bit of truth. She loved him, and she had an aching need for him buried deep inside her that somehow she must find a way to overcome.

Getting to her feet, she methodically set about her usual Friday evening routine. All the while one thought kept revolving merry-go-round-like in her mind. She remembered how Brad had said that he believed Myra knew all the facts about Howard and Sam and the past. She must ask Myra again to tell her, for if she could understand the past, then maybe she could deal with the present.

The warm June sun had caused roses to kindle along bough and bush in little flames of scarlet and bursts of flushed white and soft pink. And climbing over the trellis at the side of Myra Allan's house were masses of pale yellow roses, their light butter color blending with the pale desert sand shade of the crab orchard stone.

Myra appeared at the door as Claudia walked the short distance from the driveway to the front of Myra's house.

"I bet you could shoot me for calling up and telling you I was going to barge in on you on a Saturday afternoon like this," Claudia said in a semiapologetic voice. "But I do have to talk to you."

"Don't be silly. I'm tickled you called. Come in." Myra held the door open, stepping to one side so Claudia could enter. "I made iced tea for us. You sit down and I'll get it. Then we'll have a good visit."

While Myra was gone, Claudia glanced around at the appealing blending of colors in Myra's living room. The walls were caramel colored, and a pale salmon ceiling echoed the salmon-colored area rug that covered the waxed oak floor. The deep cushioned sofa was covered in a salmon and gray striped upholstery, and the various chairs, which picked up the caramel color of the walls mixed with accents of gray, gave the whole room a warm earthy glow.

Myra returned and took a lounge chair facing Claudia, who had taken a seat on the sofa. Claudia watched Myra as she drank a little of her tea. Perhaps it was her imagination, but Claudia thought Myra appeared somewhat uneasy with her. There had never been any restraint between them before, and she certainly didn't want there to be now.

"Myra," she commenced tentatively, "I bet you're wondering why I insisted on talking to you this afternoon." She took another taste of her tea, then set it down on a lamp table at one end of the couch. "I want to ask your help."

Myra contemplated her glass of tea without looking at Claudia. "What kind of help can I offer you?" She sounded uncertain, as if she were afraid of what Claudia might ask and therefore had reservations about it.

"It's about Brad Hayes."

Myra let her breath out audibly, looking at Claudia now with obvious relief marking her face.

"You certainly look relieved." Claudia's voice mirrored the surprise she felt at Myra's reaction. "What on earth were you expecting?"

Myra covered her throat with one hand as she shifted nervously in her chair. "I thought—I mean I felt your father might have said something about—" She hesitated, her amber eyes glistening with the sheen of tears. "Did you talk to your father today—about me, that is?"

Claudia stared at her in confusion. "No, why? If I had, what would he have told me?" She angled her head quizzically at her father's secretary. "If it's something nice about you, I want to hear it right now." She widened her eyes in an expectant smile.

Myra set her glass down and came over to sit on the sofa beside Claudia. "It's not only about me," she said, the rosy glow illuminating her face again. "Last night your father asked me to think about marrying him."

"Oh, Myra. How wonderful that would be. Dad needs you so much, and I don't know of two people more perfect for each other," Claudia exploded in an exuberant rush.

"You wouldn't mind then?"

Claudia put her arms around Myra's neck, giving her an affectionate hug. "Mind! I'm thrilled for both of you." She squeezed Myra again, then laughing happily, let her go. "You know, I believe Dad has cared for you for a long time, but he needed a little push to realize just how much. And I think maybe the same thing is true of you."

Bright tears shone in Myra's eyes and her lips parted in a soft smile. "I've been in love with Howard more years than I can count, and I never needed a push to know it. I needed patience," she said, laughing softly.

"Patience," Claudia repeated the word after her. "Is that what it takes to get the man I love to love me in return?"

Myra's expression sobered, and she inclined her head toward Claudia, eyeing her thoughtfully. "Are we talking about Brad Hayes?"

Claudia nodded, her blue-gray eyes wistful.

"Do you really believe that you're in love with him?"

"I know I am."

"Then why did you refuse to deliver the contracts to him and make me do it instead?" Myra frowned. "Let me tell you he was upset about that too. It was easy to tell that."

"I know. He came by the apartment that night, and he accused me of running out on him. He also told me that he really enjoyed talking with you. It meant a lot to him hearing the things you told him about his father. You evidently had a number of nostalgic anecdotes."

Myra scrutinized Claudia now with narrowed eyes. "I thought we were talking about your feelings for Brad, not my conversation with him about his father."

"We're talking about both," Claudia answered, raising her voice emphatically. "That's why I'm here, Myra. I have to know the real reason Dad forced Sam Hayes to take his family and leave Tulsa."

Shaking her head sadly, Myra put a sympathetic hand on Claudia's arm. "I thought you were going to ask Howard to explain that."

"I did ask him, but he never told me what I need to know." She drew her breath in slowly, then let it out in an anguished sigh. "All he said was that he did what he felt at the time he had to do in order to preserve what was important to him—our family and his company. He never would tell me any more than just that."

"It's painful for him to talk about it, even after eighteen years. You must understand that," Myra said placatingly.

"All the more reason for you to tell me," Claudia said, baiting her.

Myra rubbed one hand through her hair. "I want to ask you something. Have you told Howard that you're in love with Brad?"

"No. In fact, I told him that I wouldn't be seeing Brad

anymore now that the lease with El-Sa was signed. I knew he was relieved to hear it because it was actually what he wanted to hear. He thinks Brad will only hurt me if I let myself get involved with him even slightly.''

"And has he hurt you?"

Claudia's face knotted, her eyes seeming to grow gray and pale. "I'm hurting, all right, but I can't honestly blame it all on Brad. I knew what I was doing, but—''

"But what?"

"But he doesn't love me as I love him. I've got to find a way to come to terms with that, and I intend to." She squared her jaw, jutting her chin out in determination, then continued harshly, "To help me do it, though, I darn well need to know what it was that built an ironclad barrier between every Hayes and every Carlton." As she spoke, she bolted from her seat on the sofa and walked across the room.

Standing at the window, Claudia looked out at the wide-trunked tree in Myra's front yard. Its lush green leaves cast a circle of shade onto the grassy lawn below. She stared at the old tree as if mesmerized by its beauty, yet at the same time she was conscious of the silence in the room behind her. Either her outburst had somewhat stunned Myra, or the older woman was taking time to contemplate whether or not she should tell Claudia what she wanted to know.

Myra's caring voice broke the stillness. "You're right, you should know. Though I do feel your father should be the one to tell you, I know I can do it easier than he could." She hesitated a second before continuing. Claudia stood motionless, keeping her back toward Myra. She was actually afraid to turn or move for fear Myra might change her mind and not reveal the past to her.

"I was a spectator to all that happened, so I can be objective in telling about it and show both sides." Myra stopped again, clearing her throat before she added in a sharp-edged tone, "Actually there were three sides, and I should show them all objectively."

Claudia turned around now, looking inquiringly toward Myra. "What three? Who?"

"Howard, Sam—and Vanessa."

Color drained from Claudia's face as her body swayed forward then back as if buffeted by a blast of strong wind. "My mother played a part in this?"

"I'm afraid she did."

"Are you going to tell me that she caused what happened?" she asked, looking at Myra in dismay.

The petite, brown-haired woman nodded and at the same time extended her hand toward Claudia. "Come sit down," she said gently.

Claudia shook her head. "I can't." She clenched her hands at her sides, standing tense and still, her eyes wide and staring. "I can't do anything but pray that you're not going to tell me what I think you are." She began to tremble uncontrollably. "But you are—you are." There was a note of hysteria in her voice now. "My God! My mother was involved with Sam Hayes, wasn't she?"

"It's complicated. It's not exactly what you think."

If Myra was trying to reassure her with those words, it didn't work. Claudia covered her face with her hands, experiencing the sensation of her fingers stiff and cold against cheeks inflamed with righteous anger. Had every man she'd ever known been fair game to Vanessa?

"When you say it's not what I think, you scare me even more. I'm afraid it's even worse." Grim lines bracketed the corners of her pale mouth, deepening the shadows that hollowed her cheeks. "Just tell me, Myra—tell me please."

"All right, but it will take some explaining, and I wish you'd come sit down and listen to me."

"In a minute. I can't sit right now. I'll just stand here or walk around a little. But I'll be listening, you can bet on that." She was trying to get control of herself. Taking a few steps to bring her closer to the couch where Myra sat, Claudia thrust her hands into the slash pockets at the sides of the navy and white checked skirt she was wearing and waited for Myra to start explaining.

"Most everything at the company was going well back then in the sixties. Production was up. Sam Hayes had all of his rigs in operation for Carlton, of course, and most were having success in finding oil." She paused long enough to reach for her glass of tea, then settled back against the sofa cushions. "Your father was out of Tulsa a good deal that spring and summer. He was in Chicago and New York in order to negotiate financing for a new block of leases he'd obtained in southern Louisiana."

The sudden harsh sound of Claudia's quick intake of breath interrupted the flow of Myra's words. Myra shot her an inquiring glance.

"I'm sorry," Claudia said, frowning heavily. "Suddenly I was reminded of that line from Charles Dickens: 'It was the best of times, it was the worst of times.'" She finished with a brittle laugh.

Myra shrugged. "It was the worst for Howard when the gossip about your mother started. You know how people within a company like to talk. Especially when the boss's wife is involved."

"You mean mother was so open about this affair that people at the company knew all about it?"

"It wasn't that bad. It was just that Vanessa suddenly seemed to find a lot of excuses to come down to the office. It became a bit obvious, too, that she always managed to be around whenever Sam and the young geologist who worked for the company happened to be here to make their reports on the progress of the various wells."

"These were times when Dad was out of town, I imagine." Her tone was sarcastic, her voice bitter.

Nodding, Myra continued. "I'm sure Howard had at least heard rumors of Vanessa's appearances in the building, but it didn't all come to a head until the time he returned several days earlier than expected and discovered Vanessa had left you for two days and nights with a teenage baby-sitter."

Claudia stood behind the sofa now, running her hand along the top of the back cushions and looking down at Myra. "I don't see the connection. What does leaving me at home with a sitter have to do with Sam Hayes? Was she off someplace with him?"

"She was off driving around the drilling sites with someone. When she came home and your father confronted her about where she'd been and with whom, she named Sam."

Leaning over the back of the couch toward her, Claudia narrowed her eyes, scrutinizing Myra's face intently. "You've put that curiously. You said Vanessa named Sam, but your manner implies that you're not convinced it was he." Claudia covered her throat with her hand, swallowing hard. "Was it Sam Hayes or not?" she demanded, her voice rising shrilly.

"No it wasn't. But you see, Vanessa told Howard that she was involved with Sam and he believed her."

"Why did she lie about it?"

"Who knows for sure? I think she knew Howard would get rid of him, and she didn't want her real lover to be pushed away."

Claudia walked around to the front of the sofa and sank down at one end, leaning back with a disheartened sigh. "It was that company geologist, wasn't it?"

Myra nodded. "It was several years, however, before Vanessa ever told Howard the truth, and of course the harm had been done to Sam then and there was nothing that could remedy that."

There was a leaden grayness to Claudia's eyes as she looked thoughtfully at Myra. "It's incredibly sad, the entire tragic mess. An unfaithful wife tells one lie, and that lie harms two families and is still doing it now." A shuddering sigh caused her body to tremble. Crossing her arms, she hugged herself and ran her hands along her upper arms as if to rub warmth into them. "If only Dad had confronted Sam Hayes with mother's allegations, then Sam would have denied everything and all of the painful happenings would have been avoided."

"Don't you imagine that he regrets the actions he took against Sam more than any of us could ever realize?" Myra said, her expression as pensive as Claudia's.

"Then when he discovered the real truth, why didn't he go to Brad's father, explain the whole dreadful mistake he'd made? Heaven knows he owed Sam Hayes that at the very least." She fought to hold back her tears. "Even this late—if only Dad would tell him all of this now. Oh, Myra." Her voice broke and her eyes brimmed with tears. "Brad and his father both deserve to know. It won't change things between Brad and me, but perhaps it'll clear the muddy water to a degree."

"Then ask him." Myra leaned forward, a sound of encouragement in her voice. "Tell your father how you feel, and I'll bet that he'll do it. He'd do almost anything for you, Claudia. You know that." Myra tossed her head emphatically as she spoke, causing wisps of her brown hair to fall over her forehead.

"I don't know whether I should. If Dad has never wanted to explain things to Sam Hayes in all this time, maybe I shouldn't ask it of him now."

Myra put her hand to her brow, brushing back her hair with her fingers. "Surely you understand why Howard wouldn't explain while he was still married to Vanessa." A serious look ridged the bridge of her slender nose. "He was trying to protect her."

"After all of her infidelities," Claudia scoffed. "Why would he even try?"

"She was his wife. And what I believe was more important than that to Howard was that Vanessa was *your* mother," Myra added sternly. "Either one was reason enough. You do see that, I'm sure."

Claudia attempted to give an apologetic smile. She felt chagrined at Myra's fierce defence of her father. "You've made me see it—clearly. I want to thank you for doing it." She smiled easily now. "You do really love my dad. I'll never doubt that."

"I understand him, too," Myra said quietly.

Claudia nodded. "Apparently much better than I do."

"We both understand the problems he's faced and the hurt he's suffered."

Claudia reached over, putting her hand on Myra's. "You'll make him forget it all. With you, Dad will find the kind of happiness he's always needed."

These words stirred a luminous warmth within Myra's eyes and she sighed softly. Neither of them found any necessity of saying anything more. There was gladness in Claudia's heart knowing that a special rapport existed between her and this petite woman who was going to marry her father.

Making a show of lifting her wrist to check her watch, Claudia jumped to her feet and exclaimed about the time. "I had no idea it had gotten this late. I must go, but I appreciate your telling me all that you did. You've helped me a lot."

"I hope so." Myra stood up too, and the two of them walked toward the door. "I wish I could suggest a way to make things better for you with Brad."

"You already did. You suggested patience, remember?" Claudia said in an attempt to joke.

"If you believe that you love him, you might give it a try," Myra came back at her, a warm twinkle in her eyes.

"Patience doesn't come easy when you're twenty-two."

Myra's chin lifted at a stubborn angle. "It's no easier at thirty-nine," she mocked with a light laugh.

"You win that round, Myra," Claudia said, and with a shrug and a smile, she opened the door and stepped outside. "But you'll have to admit that there were no real barriers between you and Dad. That's not the case with Brad and me."

With a wave of her hand, Claudia hurried off to her car. As she reached the drive, she caught sight of more of Myra's yellow roses. They were cascading down the stone retaining wall that separated Myra's yard from her next-door neighbor's. All at once a painful lump rose in her throat, stopping her breath. She was re-membering pale golden roses filling a cobalt blue vase, whose beauty had been even more exquisite than the ones she was viewing now. What a shame that such fra-grant loveliness is so quick to fade and pass away, she thought.

Chapter Eleven

Less than three weeks later Alamo Drilling Company began taking truckloads of rig components weighing hundreds of thousands of pounds to the selected drill site in Stephens County for assembly.

The preparatory work was accomplished quickly through the hot and dry summer days. Three days after the drilling began, Howard stopped by Claudia's office on the pretext of wanting to tell her the latest report from the site.

"How about driving down to Stephens County with me tomorrow and see the operation for yourself?" her father asked as he stood in the doorway of her office, one hand in his trouser pocket absently jingling the change there. "Wouldn't you like that?"

"Later on maybe." She touched her finger to the cleft in her chin. "But why are you going this early? It was only yesterday that they cemented steel casing into the hole."

Howard walked on into Claudia's office, shaking his head at her and grinning at the same time. "Are you showing off how well you're keeping up with the project, or is this talk just your way of making excuses not to go with us tomorrow? You just don't want to get dirty stepping onto the floor of the drilling rig," he teased, chuckling.

She smiled and made a little face at him. "That's not it, but I would be in the way. Besides, this is a production project now. My concern with it ended when I got the leases all signed." She toyed with a pencil on her desk to avoid looking at her father. She had to think of some way to change the subject before he figured out the real reason she wouldn't go. She knew Sam Hayes had been at the drill site since before the first day of drilling. If Sam was there, it was likely that Brad was too. If he wanted to see her, he knew how to reach her. Certainly she was not going to risk running into him when he apparently had no interest in seeing her. The last time she'd heard from Brad was the night he called to tell her he was going to Calgary on business. He could still be in Canada, for all she knew. Wherever he was, he seemed to have put all thought of her out of his mind. Nervously, she kept pushing her pencil back and forth between her thumb and forefinger. Finally she looked up to see her father eyeing her thoughtfully. "Dad, the major reason that I can't take off and go with you tomorrow is that I have to be here to wind up my week's work." She talked rapidly now, wanting to veer away from any possible mention of either Brad or Sam Hayes. "I haven't told you, but I'm taking a week of my vacation beginning next week."

"You made a rather sudden decision to do that, didn't you?"

"Not really. I've been needing some time off. This is

just the first time my work schedule looked light enough to get away.''

"Hmm," he muttered, clicking his tongue against the roof of his mouth. "Do you have specific plans about where you're going?"

"I thought I'd go to the lake house. If it's okay with you, that is."

"Sure—you know it is." Her father's tone was off-hand, but his sharp blue eyes studied her face intently.

On Friday afternoon Claudia decided to leave for the lake right after work. The summer days were long, so she could go by her apartment, pick up her things and still drive to the lake house before dark.

When she got there, it looked just the way she knew it would, the setting sun leaving its heavy golden light at the edges of the sky. She unpacked her car in the lingering dusk and had herself settled by the time the sky did finally darken. She turned on the lamps in the living room and lighted the mushroom-shaped lights at the corners of the deck. Sitting outside in one of the comfortable deck chairs, she watched the fragile little moths cluster around the outdoor lights. How long she sat there in a state of relaxed reverie, she had no idea.

When she heard the sound of a night bird calling to its mate, she drew a deep, steadying breath; she now realized why she was waiting. It was like a strange revelation somehow. I'm waiting, she thought, and I've been waiting all along. Waiting for something that I'm never going to have—Brad's love.

Getting up, she moved quickly inside the house, closing and locking the sliding glass doors behind her. As she turned around and faced toward the kitchen, she saw a flash of headlights through the kitchen windows and heard the sound of a car pulling to a halt at the back of the house.

A tremor of alarm shook her. Who could be coming here tonight? No one looking for her, certainly. Other than her father, no one knew she was here at the lake. She darted across the living room into the kitchen and peered through a window at the back to see if she could make out the car and see how many people were in it. She thought it was probably someone seeking directions to another house farther up along the lakefront. She was unable to tell much of anything in the dark, and she wished she'd had the foresight to turn on the outside lights at the back door and at the corner of the house where she'd parked her car.

Hearing the car door slam, she switched on the light at the back door. A tall, straight figure approached, walking past a pair of sassafras trees between the road and the house. As he came into the lighted area, Claudia gasped in shocked surprise at the unexpected sight. It was Brad.

He must have seen her watching from the window, for he raised his hand and waved. A second later she heard his quick, loud rap on the kitchen door. "Hey, Claudia," he shouted through the closed door. "Open up. It's Brad."

It took her endless seconds to remove the chain and turn the lock because her fingers were trembling and her hands moved with jerky awkwardness. As she released the bolt, Brad turned the knob and pushed the door open so they stood facing each other.

"Hi," he said, his strong mouth smiling faintly.

Claudia could not speak. Staring at him blindly, she held on to the door as a wave of emotion washed over her.

Brad's brown eyes met her blue ones, held them for a long, electric moment. "May I come in, Claudia?"

She still held on to the door, gazing at him as if

hypnotized, taking in the tall lean look of him, his questioning eyes, his wide mouth bracketed now with grim lines. She managed finally to nod her assent. As soon as she did, he moved swiftly past her into the kitchen, turning immediately back to face her.

"I hoped you'd be happy to see me, but I'm afraid you're not."

"I'm—I'm surprised is all." Claudia let go of the door and closed it firmly behind her. "Who told you where to find me?"

"Your father."

"When did you talk to him?"

Brad took hold of both of her hands, drawing her away from the door and closer to him. "Can't we go sit down to talk about this? There's no reason we have to stand here in the kitchen, is there?" His manner was lightly teasing, which she knew was his way to ease the tension between them.

Her heart was thudding and she was suddenly aware of his nearness. His hands held hers warmly, firmly, and suddenly feelings stirred in her that she didn't want to feel.

Brad's eyes held hers and she couldn't look away. The atmosphere changed very subtly, and something surrounded them, enclosed them. Brad's face came closer, closer, and then he kissed her hungrily, holding her so close she could scarcely breathe. "Tell me you're a little glad to see me," he murmured against her lips as he eased his mouth from hers. "Because I'm so damn glad to see you. I got a terrible feeling when I was in Canada that time and distance were putting yet another barrier between us. I worked like a maniac to get the hell out of there and get back to Tulsa to be able to see you." He looked at her, something vulnerable in his face touching her even more than his words. "Tell me you're happy that I'm here," he asked her once again.

"I am, of course." She pulled away from him and walked through the kitchen to the living room. "I'm still curious though about how you found out where I was. I guess you were at the drill site today when my father was there." She tossed words at him quickly as she sat down on one of the love seats beside the fireplace. She needed to keep a little distance between them so she could get a rein on her emotions. She was still experiencing a feverish reaction to having him there with her, and she continued to feel a little dazed and breathless from being in his arms again after all these weeks. Suddenly afraid he might sit down beside her, she pointed to the other love seat. "You sit there across from me and tell me what happened."

If he sensed the reason behind her request, he gave no sign but took the seat opposite her, angling his body in a relaxed position. "I drove up from Abilene today, so I didn't get to the well until midafternoon. Your father was getting ready to leave by that time, but we talked for a few minutes. He mentioned that he'd asked you to go with him today, but you were getting things lined up to take a vacation up here at the lake."

"He knew I planned to come up tomorrow, but no one knew I was coming tonight. I didn't decide myself until I was leaving the office at five o'clock."

He observed her with a lazy smile. "That's what I figured when I got to your apartment about seven-thirty tonight and found you were gone. I took a chance on finding you here."

She raised her eyebrows in mock anger, as if he'd insulted her with an unflattering assumption. "It never occurred to you, I suppose, that some charming man had taken me out for the evening, particularly on my last night in town for a week or so."

He flashed his most engaging grin at her. "It occurred to me, all right. I considered that it more than likely was the case. I didn't enjoy the idea much, either."

"And had it been the case, then what would you have done?"

"I'd have waited here all night and greeted you when you came tomorrow," he stated, his manner totally serious.

"You're kidding me." She slanted her eyes at him, laughing. "You're too tall and long-legged to curl up like a pretzel and camp out overnight in that fancy sports car of yours."

Planting his hands on his knees, he inclined his head and shoulders toward her. "Is that right! Well, let me tell you something. I've done precisely that—more than once, I might add—sitting on a well. It's no strain when it concerns something that's important to you. And believe me, it was an important thing to me to see you."

"So important that you couldn't have waited until tomorrow and been absolutely sure I'd be here?" Claudia asked, eyeing him curiously.

"Yes," he said tersely. "I'm afraid I've already waited too long." His voice vibrated with emotion.

She stared at him, confused, her heart beating against her ribs in uneasy rhythm. What did Brad mean by his cryptic words? "I don't understand what you're getting at, Brad." She lowered her eyes and looked at her clenched hands in her lap.

"There's no way you could, because it's taken me some time to know it myself. I want to tell you everything about it though, if you'll just let me." Brad's voice sounded husky, and it sent a strange quiver all through her body.

"You—you make it sound awesome, but if it's important enough to bring you here looking for me tonight, it's important enough for me to hear it."

His eyes were shadowed and intent. "Good, but do we have to sit opposite each other like two bookends?" He got up and took two long steps to bridge the distance, then sat down on the gold shag rug, pulling her down from the love seat beside him. They sat together with their backs resting against the front of the love seat, and he gently nudged her shoulder with his and smiled suddenly. "This I like. It's a lot more friendly."

"I agree." She stretched her legs out comfortably before her, crossing them at the ankles.

Brad reached for her hand, circling his fingers firmly around hers. "Claudia, please listen to me without saying anything. It means everything to me to make sure you do understand what I want you to know."

She made a small, scarcely audible sound, drawing her shoulder slightly away from his. Fear rose like fog inside her, clouding her mind, thoughts and reason. Please God, don't let him tell me something I can't bear to hear, she prayed silently.

Brad took a deep breath, and she sensed he was as tense about what he had to tell her as she was to hear it. "I know you remember that you accused me of seeing you only as Howard Carlton's daughter. You even said that you didn't exist for me beyond that." He spoke quietly, but she felt the emotion underlining every word. She sat very still, her heart beating in a strange, irregular rhythm. She was experiencing ambivalent feelings of both hope and despair. "I hated the fact that you could say that, worse still

believe it, and you know why?'' His hand clenched hers
with a bruising fierceness. ''Because God knows I did
give you reason enough to believe it.''

She leaned forward, turning her head to look closely at
him. She observed the contorted movements of his face
and saw the same look was back in his eyes, the one that
she had seen there that morning after he had made love to
her. It froze something inside her and she wanted to cry
out, tell him not to look at her like that, but she was too
shaken to utter a sound. And besides, he'd asked her just
to listen to him without saying anything. So she stared at
him numbly, waiting, dreading what he might be going to
say next.

''In the beginning I met a beautiful, brainy petroleum
engineer and I admit I was attracted by everything about
her in those first minutes at that well site in Stephens
County. Fifteen minutes later I learned she's the daughter
of Howard Carlton, and that fact added an inescapable
dimension to the relationship before it had scarcely
begun.'' He let go of her hand and took her by the
shoulders. ''You do realize it was like that at the start,
don't you?''

She nodded, but only because he'd stopped talking and
seemed to be waiting for a sign before he would go
on.

Gently but insistently he shifted her around now,
pulling her into his arms and positioning her so that she
lay in his lap, facing him, her back supported by the leg he
kept raised behind her. In this way she was forced to look
directly into his face while he continued talking to her.
''Later, when we were getting to know each other, sailing
together and sharing the happiest and best times I've ever
known with anyone, all I thought about was how much I
wanted to make love to you. Claudia, you were the most

exciting, desirable woman I'd ever known." His fingers brushed the soft hair curling at her temples, then moved down her cheek and touched her lips. Slowly he traced the soft contours of her mouth in a way that caused a sensuous warmth to flow through her. "That time when we were here at the lake, I wanted you so much and all that mattered that night when we were together was the thrill and excitement of loving between us. Claudia—my darling Claudia," he whispered, his hands moving to take her face between them as he looked deep into her eyes. "You gave me your love and with it your beautiful, trusting vulnerability."

Claudia saw the caring in his eyes, and the infinite tenderness in his touch made tears well up, blurring her eyes.

"You're not the kind of girl a man has an affair with. You're the kind a man falls in love with and marries."

Claudia grew warm under the look in his eyes, and suddenly it seemed hard to breathe. She was very still, but she could feel her heart beating in a wild, irregular rhythm as her eyes locked with his. She couldn't move, not for anything in the world. Brad was so close to her, his hands so gentle as they held her face. Yet she wanted more. She wanted him to hold her, take her in his arms, press her close against him and tell her he loved her. The longing that filled her body was like a pain, and there was nothing that could still that pain except the words she wanted to hear. But Brad was silent now, so silent, only looking at her.

She began to tremble, as if electrified by the tension stretching taut between them. "You mean *some* man—but not you. That's what you came here tonight to tell me, isn't it? That a man named Hayes can't fall in love with Claudia Carlton."

"No, I didn't come to tell you that," he said, trailing one hand along the side of her face and then caressing the smooth skin of her throat. "It's true I did try to convince myself that I didn't and couldn't love you. That in fact a Hayes and a Carlton were like oil and water. But if I didn't love you, why was my life totally empty the minute I was no longer close enough to see you, touch you? Oh God," he groaned, suddenly gathering her up against him, her face against his chest, his mouth touching her hair. "I don't want to face the prospect of living the rest of my life without you. You're not a name; you're your own self, and I love you."

In an almost violent gesture he lifted up her face and kissed her. There was no restraint in his kiss, and Claudia trembled in his arms, overwhelmed by the emotions sweeping through her. He kissed her deeply, his hands sliding up under her hair to hold her head.

There was nothing in her mind now but the glorious fact that Brad had said he loved her, that and the sweet ecstasy of his touch. She kissed him back hungrily, losing herself in the waves of love washing over her.

He released her slowly. "Claudia, I haven't explained it all, I know," he murmured against her mouth. "And I'm sorry because I know I hurt you before. I didn't want to. I never intended to. You must believe that. Tell me you believe that," he said hoarsely.

"I do." She smiled softly, and when she did Brad quickly kissed the curved corners of her lips. "And now I want to tell you something you've been wanting to know. I did talk to Myra like you wanted me to." She placed her hands against his chest and traced the buttons on his shirt with one finger.

"I wondered if you might have." He returned her smile

and at the same time slid his hands under her, cradling her in his arms.

"Myra told me the whole story, explained the reasons my father did what he did. It's not a pretty story and I don't enjoy repeating it, but you have a right to know." Claudia closed her eyes for a second, finding it impossible to look into Brad's face while she was telling him what her mother had done. "It can't alter anything now, but maybe it will help you understand my father. He hurt all of your family, but he suffered too."

"I know already. Dad told me before I left the drilling site this afternoon to drive to Tulsa to find you."

Her eyes flew open. "You mean—my father told him? Dad explained it to Sam at last!"

"The two of them had quite a talk. I'd guess that their meeting today must have gone a long way toward clearing the air between them."

Claudia felt a sense of relief, and she pressed her head into the warm hollow of Brad's shoulder. "I hope so. It would be so good if things could be made right between our two families." She trembled, curling her fingers against the wall of Brad's chest. "Oh, Brad, I know now that your mother suffered more than anyone. I'm so sorry and I understand now just how terribly difficult it was for all of you."

"It's the past, and you and I are not going to talk about it anymore."

"What are we going to talk about then?" she asked, the smile that earlier had curved the corners of her mouth returning to put a teasing glint in her eyes.

"We're going to talk about the present because that's what concerns me. I want to talk about right now, tonight, which by the way just happens to be the first night of the beginning of my vacation. I thought you might help me decide how I should spend it.'' He looked down into her face, and his eyes held a mixture of laughter and a deeper emotion.

''I'll try, but first I'll need to know where you're going to take your vacation.''

''That depends.'' Brad's eyes darkened as they gazed down into hers and he slowly unbuttoned the top button of her dress, letting his hand skim lightly across the line of her breast.

''On what?'' Her heartbeat quickened under his touch, and she was conscious of the warm, sensual stirrings in her blood.

His hand moved gently, loosening another button. ''On where I might be invited to stay. I want to stay here with you. Do you think I could persuade you to ask me?'' He ran the back of one finger slowly along her breastbone, beneath the fabric, letting it move halfway up the rise of soft flesh, then back again.

His caress was so incredibly sensual it made her tremble and catch her breath. ''You might,'' she whispered, sighing.

''If I tell you I brought you a present, would that convince you to ask me to stay?''

''Ummm—I do love presents. What is it?''

''I'm not going to tell you. You'll have to wait and see.''

She put her hand over his to still the movement of his fingers on her breast. ''Please, Brad, where is my present? Give it to me.''

''I'll have to get it. It's in my suitcase, locked in the trunk of my car.''

She moved her head from the cradle of his shoulder. "Then don't you think you'd better get up off this rug so you can go out to your car and get it?"

He smiled, narrowing his eyes at her. "You realize, don't you, that if I bring in my luggage I'm staying."

Claudia slanted her eyes back at him. "Okay, you're staying." Her lips trembled as she added softly, "I'm asking you to, Brad."

He moved her away so he could climb to his feet, then pulled her up quickly to stand beside him. They stood there, close together yet not quite touching. Brad was looking at her so profoundly and with such love in his eyes that she raised her arms, putting them around his neck and drawing him closer to her. He bent his head and kissed her on the lips, and she could feel his heart pumping wildly against her breast.

Without a word he lifted her into his arms, carried her into her bedroom and laid her on her bed.

"Don't you move. I'll be back in less than five minutes, and I intend to take up right here where I'm leaving off." He kissed her again, this time with a fierce urgency, his arms pressed tightly across her yielding body. "Stay exactly where you are," he ordered as he strode rapidly from the room.

Claudia watched his broad shoulders and sienna-colored head disappear through the doorway. She was experiencing an overwhelming sense of euphoria. "Brad loves me," she said aloud so she could hear the wondrous sound repeated in her ears. There was a joyous sound in her voice, and she felt alive with a deep warm glowing. Brad loved her, wanted her, just as she loved and desired him. He had brought her a present and everything about this night would be perfect, magical. She let out a sigh of happiness and then narrowed her eyes curiously as she wondered what kind of gift Brad had gotten her. I bet it's something blue, she thought, and began to laugh.

"Who told you a joke while I was gone?" Brad reappeared in the doorway. He walked to the foot of the bed and stood there smiling at her with his hands hidden behind his back.

"No joke," she said, grinning up at him. "I was just laughing because I guessed something about the present you got for me."

His eyebrows arched in a look of surprise. "You have? What's that?"

"I think that, whatever it is, it's something blue. Am I right?"

He smiled. "Part of it's blue. I saw to that." His smile deepened. "And you know why I did that, don't you?"

"Because blue is my favorite color and you like to please me." She held out her hands toward him. "You also must like to tease me. But please, don't make me wait. Come here and give it to me." She wiggled her fingers at him to urge him on.

Brad walked around to the side of the bed, still keeping both his hands behind his back. "Give me your hand," he said, sitting down on the bed beside her.

Obediently, she held both her hands out palms up to receive the gift. Brad took hold of her left hand with his, turning it over deliberately yet gently. In the next moment he drew his right hand from behind him and slipped a ring on Claudia's third finger.

Claudia's eyes widened in amazement as her lips parted in an ecstatic exclamation of surprise and excitement. "Oh—oh, Brad!" She stared at the deep blue sapphire encircled with two rows of sparkling diamonds that Brad had placed on her finger. "I never dreamed you were giving me anything like this. It's the most beautiful ring I ever saw." She flung her arms around his neck. "I—I simply don't know what to say."

"Say yes, darling. It *is* an engagement ring, you know. And I did tell you that you were the special kind of girl a man falls in love with and wants to marry." He eased her back, pushing her down gently on the bed. "I do love you, Claudia, totally and completely, and I'll never stop loving you. That's something you can count on." He began to kiss her, his lips following the shape of her face, the long line of her slender neck, the warm hollow of her throat. "I'm asking you to marry me, my darling, and the sooner the better. If only you will, then I can promise you that you'll never again awaken in the morning and find me gone. I'll always be there beside you."

His arms tightened around her as he drew her close. He looked at her with infinite love and tenderness, and she could read his desire for her in his warm brown eyes and feel it in the caress of his hands.

They were two people in love, with clinging arms and seeking lips. Their lips now spoke against each other, murmuring, laughing, making small wordless sounds. "You are saying yes," Brad insisted. "Tell me you are."

A warm, fulfilling elation soared inside Claudia. She knew that she loved and was loved in return. "Yes. Oh, yes," she answered, breathing the words against his warm mouth. Then she kissed him, a long, deep kiss, pledging her heart and her love.

In the softly lighted bedroom they undressed each other, Brad's hands moving over her slender form and hers answering along the hard lines of his body. When he gathered her into his arms, her softness curved against the muscles of his chest, stomach and legs, the warmth of his body merging with hers. A soft sigh of desire came from deep inside her. "Whoever said we were oil and water was wrong, Brad, dead wrong," she said, surrounding her words with a soft, sensuous laugh.

Brad joined his low, husky laugh with hers as their lips, hands, bodies and hearts blended together.

READERS' COMMENTS ON SILHOUETTE ROMANCES:

"The best time of my day is when I put my children to bed at naptime and sit down to read a Silhouette Romance. Keep up the good work."

P.M.*, Allegan, MI

"I am very fond of the quality of your Silhouette Romances. They are so real. I have tried to read some of the other romances, but I always come back to Silhouette."

C.S., Mechanicsburg, PA

"I feel that Silhouette Books offer a wider choice and/or variety than any of the other romance books available."

R.R., Aberdeen, WA

"I have enjoyed reading Silhouette Romances for many years now. They are light and refreshing. You can always put yourself in the main characters' place, feeling alive and beautiful."

J.M.K., San Antonio, TX

"My boyfriend always teases me about Silhouette Books. He asks me, how's my love life and naturally I say terrific, but I tell him that there is always room for a little more romance from Silhouette."

F.N., Ontario, Canada

*names available on request

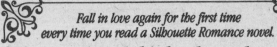

*Fall in love again for the first time
every time you read a Silhouette Romance novel.*

If you enjoyed this book, and you're ready to be carried away by more tender romance...get 4 romance novels FREE when you become a Silhouette Romance home subscriber.

Act now and we'll send you four touching Silhouette Romance novels. They're our gift to introduce you to our convenient home subscription service. Every month, we'll send you six new Silhouette Romance books. Look them over for 15 days. If you keep them, pay just $11.70 for all six. Or return them at no charge.

We'll mail your books to you two full months *before they are available anywhere else.* Plus, with every shipment, you'll receive the Silhouette Books Newsletter absolutely free. *And Silhouette Romance is delivered free.*

Mail the coupon today to get your four free books—and more romance than you ever bargained for.

Four exciting

First Love from Silhouette

romances yours for 15 days—*free!*

These are the books that girls everywhere are reading and talking about, the most popular teen novels being published today. They're about things that matter most to young women, with stories that mirror their innermost thoughts and feelings, and characters so real they seem like friends.

To show you how special First Love from Silhouette is, we'd like to send you or your daughter four exciting books to look over for 15 days—absolutely free—as an introduction to the First Love from Silhouette Book Club℠ If you enjoy them as much as we believe you will, keep them and pay the invoice enclosed with your trial shipment. Or return them at no charge.

As a member of the Club, you will get First Love from Silhouette books regularly—delivered right to your home. Four new books every month for only $1.95 each. You'll always be among the first to get them, and you'll never miss a title. There are never any delivery charges and you're under no obligation to buy anything at any time. Plus, as a special bonus, you'll receive a *free* subscription to the First Love from Silhouette Book Club newsletter!

So don't wait. To receive your four books, fill out and mail the coupon below *today!*

First Love from Silhouette is a service mark and registered trademark.

FL-OP-A